He looked up at her suddenly. "I'm your friend. I'll always be on your side."

And that was all he'd ever be if she let this go now. The thought opened up a whole world of regret. Taking all of her courage into her hands, she stepped toward Will and stood on her toes to kiss his cheek.

Their bodies never touched, and Will didn't move. But fire ignited in his eyes, the kind that could suck all of the oxygen from a room.

"Are you telling me that you want to take this slow?"

"Yes. Slow gives us both the chance to work out what we really want. We're both so different…"

"We can be different. And I can do slow."

Lark really wished he hadn't said that, because now the craving for his touch was becoming unbearable. She leaned forward, kissing him on the lips, and this time he responded, his fingers light on her cheek as he kissed her back.

Dear Reader,

Could you change places with your best friend? I'm not sure I could, but that's what's being asked of Will and Lark. And they're discovering a lot—not just about each other but about themselves. Are they really as different as they'd thought? And is their friendship something that's set in stone, or might it blossom into a love affair?

Reassessing their work roles is daunting enough, but the real challenge for Lark and Will is when they find themselves questioning everything they've taken for granted about their own lives. After four years of feeling that they're on sure ground together, anything might happen. They both have a great deal to gain, but there's a lot to lose as well.

Every hero and heroine I write has a place somewhere in my heart, and I admire Will and Lark for their courage. Thank you for reading their story, and I hope that you enjoy it!

Annie x

HEALED BY HER RIVAL DOC

ANNIE CLAYDON

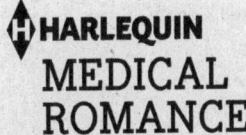

If you purchased this book without a cover you should be aware that this book is stolen property. It was reported as "unsold and destroyed" to the publisher, and neither the author nor the publisher has received any payment for this "stripped book."

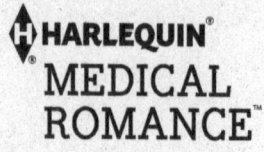

ISBN-13: 978-1-335-59502-7

Healed by Her Rival Doc

Copyright © 2023 by Annie Claydon

All rights reserved. No part of this book may be used or reproduced in any manner whatsoever without written permission except in the case of brief quotations embodied in critical articles and reviews.

This is a work of fiction. Names, characters, places and incidents are either the product of the author's imagination or are used fictitiously. Any resemblance to actual persons, living or dead, businesses, companies, events or locales is entirely coincidental.

For questions and comments about the quality of this book, please contact us at CustomerService@Harlequin.com.

Harlequin Enterprises ULC
22 Adelaide St. West, 41st Floor
Toronto, Ontario M5H 4E3, Canada
www.Harlequin.com

Printed in U.S.A.

Cursed with a poor sense of direction and a propensity to read, **Annie Claydon** spent much of her childhood lost in books. A degree in English literature followed by a career in computing didn't lead directly to her perfect job—writing romance for Harlequin—but she has no regrets in taking the scenic route. She lives in London, a city where getting lost can be a joy.

Books by Annie Claydon

Harlequin Medical Romance

The Best Man and the Bridesmaid
Greek Island Fling to Forever
Falling for the Brooding Doc
The Doctor's Reunion to Remember
Risking It All for a Second Chance
From the Night Shift to Forever
Stranded with the Island Doctor
Snowbound by Her Off-Limits GP
Cinderella in the Surgeon's Castle
Children's Doc to Heal Her Heart
One Summer in Sydney

Visit the Author Profile page at Harlequin.com for more titles.

For Richard

**Praise for
Annie Claydon**

"A spellbinding contemporary medical romance that will keep readers riveted to the page, *Festive Fling with the Single Dad* is a highly enjoyable treat from Annie Claydon's immensely talented pen."

—*Goodreads*

CHAPTER ONE

'My apologies... After you.'

On a wet Monday morning, in a crowded coffee shop, those cheerful tones could only belong to one person. Everyone else here was focused on getting to work, and didn't have time for pleasantries.

'I'm so sorry, did I spill coffee on you? I really should have looked where I was going,' a woman's voice replied.

Dr Will Bradley was probably giving a 'no matter' shrug right now, which indicated that even if she had he wasn't going to take it personally.

'It's nothing. Have a great day.'

Lark Foster heard the woman laugh. 'You too.'

She turned, to see Will joining the end of the queue behind her. She motioned to the man between them to take her place, and Will gave her the smile that he specialised in. The one that made everyone in receipt of it feel as if they were the only person in the room, and always seemed to bring out the best in people.

'Good weekend?'

'Yes, thanks.' Lark grinned back at him, because even after four years of working with Will it was impossible not to react to his effortless invitation to see the nicer side of life.

When the handsome, charming neurologist had joined the staff of Migraine Community Action, working alongside Lark at the charity for two days a week, she'd had three reservations. Handsome—gorgeous, actually—was hard to ignore, but determination could work wonders, and Lark had no time for that kind of distraction. Will's charm was a difficulty, because it was always difficult to tell what he was really thinking. And a consultant neurologist? Lark had been assured that their jobs for the remaining three days a week were irrelevant to their equal status at the charity, but wouldn't he take it for granted that his opinion would carry more weight than that of a paramedic?

Will had put that concern to rest straight away. On his first day he'd mentioned the paper she'd written on childhood migraine, and asked several questions that betrayed a genuine interest in her work. He didn't expect her to defer to him, and he never deferred to her either, assuming that as equals she'd make her case as well as he could.

She reached forward, brushing a drop of coffee from the sleeve of his raincoat. 'I see you had a good weekend too.' No one, not even Will, apologised when someone spilled coffee on them, unless they were in a good mood.

'Right in one, Sherlock.' The smile slipped from Will's face. Clearly the good part of his weekend hadn't been as effortless as he liked to make out. 'I popped in to the hospital to see Howard yesterday.'

This was what Lark shared with Will. As their friendship had grown, Will had started to smile a little less when he was with her, coming out from behind his barrage of charm to tell her what was really on his mind. That was what made *her* feel special, because it was something that Will didn't bestow on just anyone.

'I heard from Alyssa, that you did a little more than just pop in.' Lark had spent some time on the phone with Howard's wife on Sunday evening, to see how she was coping.

Will shrugged off his own good deeds, as if they meant no more than a drop of coffee. 'He's still very frustrated over not being able to tell us everything that he thinks we need to know, so we can keep things running smoothly.'

Lark nodded. Howard's stroke had struck like

a bolt out of the blue, a healthy, vigorous man in his early sixties, suddenly partially paralysed on the right side of his body and affected by expressive aphasia, which meant he could read and understand the spoken word, but speaking and writing were major challenges for him right now. One source of his frustration was that the charity he'd founded twenty-five years ago, where Lark and Will worked as joint seconds-in-command, could no longer rely on his guiding hand.

'I don't know how I'd manage. Knowing exactly what I want to say and not being able to say it.'

'Yeah. Particularly for someone like Howard, who knows how everything works, and keeps a lot of it filed away in his head. I told him you'd been through everything on his desk...'

Lark turned the corners of her mouth down. 'I don't expect he liked that very much.'

Will's smile, again. This time it wasn't just the random good humour that he shared with everyone but had a point to it. 'Howard understands that we have to go through everything and pick up what needs to be done while he's away. You have to leave him the option of not liking it very much, even if he knows you're doing a great job.'

It was good to hear someone say that. Everyone else at the charity had made jokes about venturing into the lion's den, but Will had stayed late with her after work, quietly keeping her supplied with mugs of tea and some very nice home-made biscuits that he'd obtained from somewhere, while Lark sorted through correspondence and to-do lists, trying to make sense of it all, and hoping she hadn't missed anything.

'I don't suppose he mentioned the Board of Trustees?' They'd been suspiciously quiet over the last week, and not one of them had set foot in the charity's offices.

'He did, actually. They're there to guide and help us but it's up to us to keep things running. We make decisions together, as we always have, and the only difference is that we have to do it without Howard to help us.'

'He didn't *say* all that, did he?' Lark smirked at Will.

'No, I started off with a set of Yes/No options and we worked from there. I read it all back to him and asked if it was correct, and he gave me an emphatic thumbs-up. He may not be able to put things into words at the moment, but he still knows what he wants.'

Lark nodded. 'Alyssa said that he's starting to speak a little now.'

'A few words, yes and no mainly, and some

names. He's getting to grips with different sounds, and names that begin with *M* are easiest at the moment, so we'll both have to wait our turn. It's a lot of hard work for him and I'd be tearing my hair out in his shoes.'

They'd reached the head of the queue, and he turned to the young woman behind the counter, who grinned back at him as she suddenly found herself the only person in the room.

'A cappuccino and a black coffee, both large, please.' Will shot her a twinkle from his baby-blue eyes. He might be tall, dark-haired and handsome, but it was the softness of his eyes that caught people's attention, every time.

'And a chocolate croissant...' Lark nudged Will and he nodded.

'Make that two croissants, please.' Before Lark could get out her purse, Will had produced a note from his wallet, telling her that it must be his turn to pay.

Lark had known Howard ever since she'd first come to London, when he was a tutor for her university course in Paramedic Science, running the charity from home in his spare time. When he'd taken the step of renting a dark and not particularly welcoming space on the top floor of a solid building in central London, she'd been one of the students who'd turned up to help with the painting, and her interest in childhood migraine meant that she'd become a regular volunteer with Migraine Community Action.

Now the space was unrecognisable, a light, cream-painted space divided up by glazed walls, which conveyed accessibility and calm. With offices on one side and a large clinic on the other, the charity's staff had one central hub for their activities. As the operation had expanded, Howard had offered Lark a job, and a year later he'd recruited Will.

Will had brought his own stamp to the area that greeted them when the lift doors opened. He'd consulted his never-ending contacts list and managed to persuade a range of artists to work for free in support of a good cause. The artwork on the walls lent an air of sophistication, tempered by a touch of quirky humour, and a few practical suggestions from Lark had brought it all together beautifully. Visitors often commented on the stylish and welcoming feel of the space, and the people who worked here had been pleased and proud when a leading interiors magazine had run a feature on the low-cost, high-impact transformation.

'Your place or mine?' Will couldn't help a slight quirk of his lips as he asked the question, and Lark ignored the idea that he probably had plenty of practice with it. That was his business, and here it was an easy-going, unchallenging query about where they would drink their coffee and discuss the upcoming week, before anyone else arrived.

'Yours. Take the coffee and I'll go and see if the helpline staff had a chance to sort the post over the weekend.'

The call logs were in her pigeonhole, and she scanned them, noting that nothing was marked for her or Will's attention. The helpline had clearly been busy and the post was unsorted, so she picked up the bundles of envelopes, taking them through to Will's office.

Will was sitting on one of the two large sofas in his office, already in his shirtsleeves, the coffee and croissants laid out on the bulky coffee table that separated the sofas. His desk was pushed into an alcove in one corner, and was scrupulously tidy, largely because he very seldom sat at it. As far as Will was concerned, ergonomic seating and a large computer screen took second place to sprawling on the sofa with his laptop.

He sprang to his feet, taking her raincoat and hanging it up next to his. 'Did you have any thoughts about staffing while Howard's away, over the weekend?'

'Yes, I did. If Carole's willing to work three

days instead of two, then it would be really helpful if she could take over the accounting. And you said that Dev's happy to cover for Howard in the office and with any medical questions from Tuesday to Thursday?'

Will nodded. 'Yes, he said that's no problem. In fact, three days in the office, plus being available during the evenings to liaise with us, suits him a great deal better than the five days a week doing home visits that he does at the moment. He'll be home a lot more and I think his wife could do with some extra help with the new baby.'

'Let's do that, then.' Lark sat down, dumping the post onto the table.

'You don't think that we should change our days? I could adjust my schedule and cover a couple of days when you're not here.' Will took a gulp of his coffee and started to sort through the post.

'No, the whole office structure's designed to be flexible and it runs itself most of the time. Dev will be here mid-week to give everyone the confidence of having someone to go to if they need it and our clinics are already fixed for Mondays and Fridays. I think we'll be better off working together on the policy and decision-making we'll have to do while Howard's away.'

These were the roles they'd settled into. Lark was a facilitator while Will dealt with ideas, and the reason they were so effective as a team was that they each saw the importance of the other's way of working.

Will gave her his you're-the-only-person-in-the-room smile. It had somehow become much more effective since they'd had to deal with the worry of Howard's stroke.

'You don't think we ought to take a break from each other, then?'

It felt good to laugh with him over it. 'I'll let you know if things get to that, Will.'

Wordlessly, they fell into the usual Monday morning ritual of glancing through their post while they drank coffee. Lark's pile of opened letters grew steadily, while Will seemed to have got stuck on the first of his, reading through the pages and then taking a gulp of his coffee before he went back to the beginning to read it all again.

'What's that?' Whatever the letter contained, Will didn't look too pleased about it.

'It's...' He shook his head, reaching across to sort through her letters and picking one out of the pile. 'You have one as well. This is outrageous...'

'Okay.' Lark could take outrageous or amazing, or any other extreme that Will came up with, and turn his flair and creativity into a practical proposition.

'No, I mean… It actually *is* outrageous. Read it.'

The letter was typed on the charity's headed notepaper and signed by the Chair of the Board of Trustees. Lark read it through carefully, with a growing sense of horror. For once, outrageous was an understatement.

'They want us to…*what*…?'

Will nodded. 'Yep. Sir Terence isn't satisfied with the two of us working together as we usually do to run the charity while Howard's away. He thinks we should explore the possibility of one of us stepping into his shoes on a temporary basis…'

'Which isn't going to work, because we both have other jobs.' That had always been important to Howard, he wanted the charity's employees and policy-makers to retain an ongoing involvement in treating patients with the NHS. It worked well, and Lark couldn't imagine why Sir Terence was now trying to fix something that wasn't broken.

'Exactly. I'm not in a position to give up my job, even if I wanted to, and I doubt you feel any differently. And this…' He jabbed his finger at the first paragraph on the second page, which had made Lark swallow hard when she'd read it.

'Since we have very different roles here, he wants each of us to consider how well we'd be able to take on overall responsibility...' Lark turned the corners of her mouth down, numbness beginning to take over from shock. 'That opens a whole can of worms.'

'Too right it does. They have two people who already work together well... We *do* work together well, don't we?'

'Yes. I couldn't do what you do...'

'And I wouldn't know where to begin with what you do.' Warmth flashed in Will's eyes. 'And they've chosen now—when we're having to manage without Howard—to ask us to experiment with reversing those roles. Instead of asking us what we need, and trying to help, which would be much more to the point.'

Lark nodded in agreement. 'It's not helpful at all. This last paragraph...' She flipped the paper with her finger.

Sir Terence had worked his way around to what he really wanted to say in the last paragraph, and everything that was implicit in the rest of the letter was horrifyingly explicit here. This was a time of change and they should embrace it. She and Will were in competition, not just to show how well they could do each other's jobs, or even for the post of temporary Chief

Executive, but to gain Sir Terence's backing to succeed Howard when he retired.

'He's assuming Howard *will* retire. I think he's got a lot more left to do.'

'So do I. No one's going to write him off without a fight from me.' Will threw the letter down onto the coffee table. 'Do you suppose Alyssa knows about this?' Howard's wife was a GP and had been involved with the charity from the very start, and she brought a great deal of expertise and common sense to her role as a trustee.

'She would have said something when I spoke to her yesterday. And we mustn't involve her, Will, she's got enough on her plate at the moment.'

Will nodded in agreement. 'Well, I'm going to call Sir Terence and tell him that this isn't on. He can't move us around like pieces on a chessboard, to see what happens.'

He jumped to his feet, making for the phone on his desk. Things were getting very serious.

'Wait… Will, wait. It's eight in the morning and you know that Sir Terence is usually at his desk between nine and twelve. That's the best time to call him.'

'Interrupting his breakfast or, better still, hauling him out of bed, will no doubt convince him that this is a very poor idea. And that he needs to row back on it immediately.'

This was why Lark generally called Sir Terence, when Howard wasn't available to speak to him. The Board of Trustees might love Will's ideas, but they loved them best when she outlined them, after having added a few practical adjustments.

'Stop, Will. I've got another idea.'

He smiled suddenly, returning to his seat. 'Okay. Hit me with it...'

'We do what we've always done, with every challenge. We work together. The only way that we get to be in competition with each other is if we allow that to happen.'

Will thought for a moment. 'You mean play Sir Terence at his own game?'

'Not entirely. I mean go along with it and make it ours. Show him that we're a strong enough team to address anything that's thrown at us. I reckon that's far more effective than objecting to a situation that he's trying to put us in.'

'And this management consultant who's supposed to be coming in to see us?'

'Same thing. We put up a united front and make it work for us. Who knows, we might actually learn something from switching roles?'

'I already know I couldn't do what you do.'

Lark felt the warmth of a blush begin to rise to her cheeks. She'd always thought it a little odd that Will's you're-the-only-other-person-in-the-room brand of charm still worked when she actually *was* the only other person in the room.

'And who knows where exploring that would lead?'

Asking Will to plunge into something and find out where it led was always like a red rag to a bull. He seemed to relax suddenly, savouring the idea.

'And one big advantage of that is that we don't rock the boat. If Howard gets wind of this and thinks we're unhappy with it, then he'll just start to worry even more than he is already. If we can just take it all in our stride, then it's not an issue.'

Lark nodded. 'That's what I'm thinking. So we do as we're intending with everything else, and make this work. When Howard gets out of hospital he'll be in rehab for about six weeks, so for that time at least we need to fight our own battles, and do it together and in our own way.'

Will leaned back against the sofa cushions, regarding her thoughtfully. A little tingle ran down Lark's spine. Already they were negotiating new challenges together, and even stepping that far out of their roles was surprisingly confronting. Deliciously so, actually, as if she was seeing Will anew.

'Yes, we can do that. We'll make this okay.'

Lark wasn't entirely sure that they could. But in Will's mind *okay* was the polar opposite of *outrageous,* and it was her preferred option as well.

'Agreed then?'

'Yes, agreed. You always *were* the voice of reason, Lark. We'll let Sir Terence have his breakfast in peace, shall we?'

Nightingales were overrated. Will had had his share of dates that had ended on the pavement that ran around Berkeley Square, and he'd swept his partner into a few dance steps, crooning the words of the old song into her ear. They'd ended with laughter and a kiss and sometimes a little more...

But the lark, whose song Romeo and Juliet had so dreaded in the warmth of the night... The lark was something different. A songbird of the morning, whose brown plumage became shot with gold in the sunshine, in much the same way that Lark's hair and eyes did. If he'd dared to mention nightingales to her at midnight, somewhere in the vicinity of Berkeley Square, she would have laughed and waved down a taxi, leaving him with a more authentic warmth to take home with him.

She was practical, all-seeing, and she was the only woman that Will had ever met who teased him so deliciously. Their friendship had been cemented when she'd reproved him for gaining everyone's agreement to a project that they'd jointly proposed, with the help of a couple of well-chosen quotes from Shakespeare and a smile.

'Charm takes you a very long way, Will. But what happens if the figures don't stack up?' Lark had waved a copy of her carefully thought-out spreadsheet at him.

'If we're going to be strictly practical, then none of it stacks up. All that we do is based on the premise of commitment and passion.'

Lark had considered the matter for a moment. *'I suppose so. Maybe I'll just have to get used to the idea that no one likes facts and figures quite as much as sweeping ideas.'*

Will had begged to differ on that, and they'd ended up laughing about it. Lark was charming in a way that he could never be, and he never tired of watching her mind work, sorting and clarifying until an idea so thin that it was practically translucent became something solid and workable. The slight furrow of her brow, the twist of her lips as she called him out on the flaws in his logic.

Their strength was in their differences. Together they were a force to be reckoned with, but it was with a trace of regret that Will admitted to himself that there was one thing they'd never be able to do. They'd never welcome the call of the nightingale, in the velvet darkness of an embrace.

Lark had suggested that they start as they meant to go on and write a joint letter of reply to the Board of Trustees. Will had agreed to draft one up, and he'd emailed his first thoughts through to her so they could review them over sandwiches at lunchtime.

She read the letter through carefully, voicing her approval of a couple of the points he'd made and suggesting a few improvements elsewhere.

'I left my favourite quote out…'

'Good choice. It's a great quote and very appropriate, but in this instance it's our own words that are important.'

This wasn't like the fleeting pleasure of a kiss. Lark made him feel good in an entirely different way, one that took up residence somewhere in his consciousness.

He called up the document on his laptop and made the changes that Lark had suggested, before hitting the print button. They both added their signatures, side by side at the bottom of the letter, in a gesture that felt a lot like a plunge into unknown waters.

'So we'll see what this Management Consultant has to say for himself on Friday.' Will fetched an envelope from his desk, folding the letter into it and sealing it.

'I suppose so.' Lark took one moment to frown and then turned her mind to the present. 'In the meantime, it's business as usual. You're free for the two new referrals this afternoon?'

Will nodded. They'd started to see new referrals to the charity's clinic together, before discussing which of them would take on the lead role in each patient's care. Lark had suggested that it might save a lot of time further down the line, in terms of liaison and briefing each other, and she'd been right.

'Yep. You fancy dinner this evening?' That was one nice thing about their relationship being firmly rooted in friendship. Will could ask Lark to dinner, knowing that she took it solely as an invitation to eat.

'That would be really nice. Some time out of the office to sit back and review things.'

Will chuckled. 'Right. Don't bring your laptop, it'll spoil the mood.'

CHAPTER TWO

WILL SEEMED TO be taking all of this in his stride. There were times when Lark envied his commitment to ideas, and his blithe certainty that awkward details would shrivel in the heat of what was indisputably right. All they knew about the Management Consultant who would be visiting on Friday afternoon was his name—Pete Mason—and not knowing what their upcoming meeting would entail made it difficult for Lark to plan for it. That made her very nervous.

The meeting took longer than the expected hour, which was an annoyance, since Will and Lark had had to reschedule a couple of other appointments to make time for it. By the time they'd finished the office was empty and Will unlocked the glazed doors which led out into the lift lobby and shook Pete's hand.

'Thanks. Plenty of food for thought...'
Pete nodded. 'I'll see you next Friday?'

'Looking forward to it.' Will glanced at Lark and she nodded. They watched Pete into the lift, and as the doors closed they turned to face each other.

'He's thorough. I'll give him that…' Will puffed out a breath, the smile disappearing from his face.

'This isn't what we signed up for, Will.' Pete had employed all of the techniques of a counsellor, which Lark recognised because she'd used a few of them herself with her own patients. Listening, asking questions.

'No, it's not. Although, in truth, management is a lot about personalities.'

'That's not the point. How we operate at work is fair game, but this is clearly an exercise in delving into our personal lives.' Lark turned the corners of her mouth down.

Will understood immediately what was nagging at her. 'You mean all of the questions about Robyn.'

Lark's younger sister. An accident when Robyn was five years old had left her legs partially paralysed, and when she'd landed a place at art school in London their parents had vetoed the idea of Robyn studying so far from home. Robyn's adventurous spirit had clashed head-on with their parents' protective instincts and everyone had appealed to Lark, who had just qualified as a paramedic, to speak to everyone else and talk some sense into them.

It had felt a lot like being a peace negotiator in a war-torn province. They'd all had to give a little, love a lot. But Lark had liaised with the college that had offered Robyn a place, and found a ground floor flat that was suitable for wheelchair use and gave easy access to the campus. When their parents had driven away, leaving the sisters together in their new home, she and Robyn had hugged each other, both talking excitedly about the adventures ahead of them.

They'd both worked hard and supported each other. Lark had been able to save enough to afford a deposit and bought a bungalow in the London suburbs, which gave her and Robyn more room than they'd had in the flat. Of course, it hadn't all been plain sailing. Helping Robyn to gain her independence and land a good job had provided a few challenges. In the six years that she and Robyn had lived together, they'd both changed. Both learned a bit, because that was what you were supposed to do when faced with a new phase in life.

'My home situation *does* have some bearing on the way I work, I suppose...'

Will's brow darkened. 'Maybe. Everything we do influences us in some way. But I wasn't happy with the question about whether you feel you're trying to recreate a caring situation at work because that's the one you had at home.'

Will had said as much during the session, coming to her defence with an unusual burst of anger. Lark had appreciated that, even if it wasn't strictly necessary, and she'd been forced to wonder whether Pete had a point.

'I do miss having Robyn around, now that she's married…' Lark could admit to that now that she wasn't under Pete's calculating gaze.

'Not the same thing. You miss Robyn as your sister, or as a wheelchair user?'

Will's questions were just as pointed as Pete's had been but they came from a different place. One of knowing her and Robyn.

'Right now, we could do with her as a volunteer.' Lark looked over at the empty reception area, which Robyn had presided over for a couple of evenings every week, dispensing the same kindness and understanding to their patients as she had when they were children and the migraine headaches had brought Lark to a standstill.

'Yeah, me too.' Will grinned. 'I dare say she would have made some comment to Pete about us being too busy for his session to have overrun. I'm rather regretting that she and Matt live so far away…'

He always made her laugh, even through the

most difficult and confusing times. 'That would have been nice.'

'Look, you cared for your sister because she's your sister, and Robyn cared for you in return.' Will turned the corners of his mouth down. 'It's very easy to take one look at people and assign roles, particularly with families. The truth's a bit more complicated and takes work.'

His face had darkened, and this was clearly something that Will felt strongly about. Lark raised her eyebrows in a silent question, and Will shook his head in a wordless answer. Sometimes—just sometimes—Lark got the impression that there were things that Will never talked about, even to her. Suddenly he smiled, and the moment of asking was lost.

'I'm perfectly aware of who's boss around here.'

'That would be Howard.'

He let out a derisive laugh. 'Yeah, right. How many times has he said that he defers to your good sense?'

'And how many times has he said that we depend on your ideas?'

'So he's a great boss. An idea isn't much good unless you can put it into practice, Lark. You're the glue that holds this place together, and that's true leadership.'

It was nice to hear Will say that, because the

meeting with Pete had given Lark the feeling that, in the nicest possible way, she was being attacked and undermined. A tear rolled down her cheek, and she shrugged it away.

But Will always knew how to make people feel better about things, and it appeared that Lark wasn't entirely immune to his talents. When he stepped forward, curling his arm around her shoulder and hugging her, he made her feel much, much better.

She knew all about his touch already. They'd spent the last four years bumping into each other in corridors, Will had caught her a couple of times when she'd tripped, and Lark had lost count of the number of times she'd grabbed his arm to prevent Will from acting on an impulse that they hadn't thought through yet. Will had even brushed his lips against her cheek at the Christmas party. But none of that was like this. A sudden feeling of warmth that held nothing of the everyday, but was an exquisite, one-time token of friendly affection.

And she'd just learned that Will was a really great hugger. He didn't hold her too tight, but somehow he took her breath away. Not clinging or intrusive but there for her, letting her sink into the heat that was suddenly surrounding her.

'What are we going to do, then?' She took the

risk of laying her head against his shoulder, and realised that his heart was beating fast. Even that made her feel better, as if his every instinct was readying him to come to her defence.

'We'll do what we said we would, even if I noticed you weren't entirely convinced...'

'Neither were you.'

Will's chuckle was even more enticing when she could feel as well as hear it. She should probably step away from him now, but this was far too nice to do anything of the sort. Even if it probably meant a great deal more to her than it did to him.

'I must be slipping. I was doing my best to put my doubts aside and not give too much away. Look, he's outlined the different roles that he supposes we fit into, and asked us to swap...'

'He's not entirely wrong, we are very different.'

'He *is* entirely wrong, because he reckons that our roles confine us instead of empowering us. And now it's just you and me, we'll do things our way, as you suggested.'

Lark nodded. Will sounded so certain that they weren't confined by their roles and she'd take his word for it until she'd worked the idea through in her head. 'And *our way* is?'

'We have a way of working here that benefits the charity and our patients, and I don't think we should meddle with that right now. But we could have some fun with it, and get to know each other's weekends a little better, couldn't we? If that informs our work roles then so be it.'

Lark thought for a moment. Spending a weekend with Will sounded... Delicious. That probably wasn't what Pete had been thinking, and she shouldn't think that way either.

'So... I'll spend a weekend going out and sweet-talking everyone I meet...?' Possibly taking someone home for a night of sweet romance, even. There was a problem with that, because the last few years hadn't given her much time for the complex negotiations that starting a relationship required. Although Will didn't seem to need that, his relationships might only have a shelf life of about a month, but there were enough of them.

He knew what she was thinking, and his face took on a look of gentle reproach. 'See how little you really know me?'

She couldn't resist that temptation. 'Okay. Surprise me, then. And I'll surprise you, maybe.'

Lark couldn't help squeezing him a little tighter and she felt Will catch his breath. Too much. It was too sweet, too comforting, and she was suddenly far too aware of his body. This was a world away from being able to tease him about keeping in shape, and a mere whisper away from testing out every movement and reaction. She patted his shoulder and stepped back.

Even that was delicious. The look in Will's eyes made her feel that she was the only person in the universe. There was understanding, warmth, and the slightest trace of regret that the moment was over. And it *was* over, because Lark wasn't sure she could risk doing that again.

'Okay, so this weekend I have to be at my parents' cocktail evening in aid of a hospice that's local to them. *Next* weekend's the evening they're holding in support of Migraine Community Action, that Howard and I were going to go to. I can't do that alone.'

Lark reckoned he probably could. She'd seen Will work a room, and decided on the spot that she was better off sticking with what she was good at. 'I don't have anything quite so glittering planned.'

He grinned. 'That's all in the eye of the beholder. Parties can lose their shine if you go to enough of them…'

The coffee shop was always busy at seven on a Monday morning. People deciding to make an early start and vanquish the coming week before it could throw anything in their way. As Lark held the glass door open for someone who was exiting with their coffee, the sight of Will's broad shoulders at the end of the queue made her feel a lot more confident about the vanquishing part of the week.

'Hey...' She tapped him on his right shoulder, ducking around to his left side and waiting until Will looked back at her. Worked every time.

'There you are...' He always made their first greeting of the day sound as if it were something special that he'd been waiting for. This morning that produced an unusual quiver that ran deliciously down her spine.

'You look a little weary.' Will was showing definite signs of a couple of very late nights, and Lark swallowed down the impulse to demand to know what he'd been up to. *That* was new, too.

'Yeah. It was my mother's birthday yesterday and we made a thing of it.'

The Bradley family made a thing of everything. William Bradley senior did a lot of entertaining in connection with his mechanical engineering company, and Priscilla Bradley worked hard for a carefully selected list of charities. Lark and Robyn had been to a New Year's celebration held at his parents' large house in Hertfordshire, and Lark had been astonished that one couple could know so many people.

'She had a nice day?'

'She had a great day.' Will narrowed his eyes.

'I suppose you could always mention Dad's parties to Pete. If he thinks you're trapped in a role that's dictated by your family, he'd have a field day with mine.'

Will's family *were* fertile ground, if you had a mind to look at it that way. People often commented on how different the three brothers were, Will handsome and charming, Edward quiet and businesslike and Joel the academic. Of course that didn't take account of Will's ferocious intellect and his years of study to become a doctor, or the fact that he could advise his patients calmly and precisely when he wanted to.

'I'm not going to get Pete off my back by focusing his attention on you.'

'That's very noble of you.' Will grinned at her.

'So how was the party?'

'Great. Some really interesting people there. I got distracted, though, and ended up in the kitchen, talking until two in the morning.'

'Was she nice?' Lark felt her heart sink, as if it had suddenly taken on more weight than it could handle.

'Gorgeous. Amazing, actually, and very interesting. Emma...' He grinned as Lark's eyebrows shot up.

'I thought a gentleman never tells.' She heard a cool edge creep into her tone, and pressed her lips closed. Will's conquests had never particularly bothered her before now.

'It depends what there is to tell. Miss Emma Salisbury.'

'You mean...*the* Emma Salisbury?' One half of the Salisbury sisters who had taken a small local newspaper and transformed it into a popular and well-regarded national publication. Emma was the eldest, and must be in her eighties.

'Yep. Fascinating woman. She was telling me about how, by coincidence, she'd been in America when JFK was assassinated. She drove all the way to Texas in a beat-up old Chevy, and her pictures and interviews formed the basis of the book that she and her sister produced some years later.'

'I hear it's a wonderful book.' *Witnesses* concentrated on the reactions of ordinary people who had been caught up in world-changing events, and had won a string of literary and journalistic prizes.

'Yes, it is. When I saw the guest list I looked out my copy and put it into the car, in case I had a chance to ask her to sign it for me. She was very gracious.' Will tapped his briefcase, in an indication that he'd brought the now precious book to show her. 'I took up far too much of her time, but she said that these days she prefers sandwiches and cocoa in the kitchen to kicking up her heels.'

That was Lark's go-to position, as well. 'I don't blame her.'

'Me neither.' He grinned at Lark's raised eyebrows. 'Sometimes my father's expectations do get a little heavy to carry. So what did *you* get up to at the weekend?'

Lark shrugged. 'Not a great deal. I spent Saturday afternoon with Howard, and he's in good form. He was showing off some of the words he's been working on with his speech therapist. Alyssa says he'll be moving into rehab soon.'

'That's great. Good for him.'

'And I chose some paint for my sitting room…' Lark dredged up the only other thing she'd done that was even vaguely remarkable.

'Yeah? What colour…?'

Will had somehow contrived to make Lark's weekend sound more interesting than his own, and by the time they reached the office he'd started to interrogate her about the lighter shades she had in mind for the ceiling. He broke off as the phone rang, and Lark leaned over the reception desk to answer the call.

'Hello, Migraine Community Action. How can we help you?'

'My name's Stan Copeland. It's my wife, Sandra...' The voice on the other end of the line sounded ragged and stressed. 'She came to see you at one of your clinics...'

Lark thought for a moment. 'I remember—I saw Sandra a few weeks ago, didn't I. How is she now?'

'She's been following the advice you gave and she's been much better. But over the weekend—she's had the most dreadful headache that she just can't shake. I called the doctor this morning and he said that it might be stress—Sandra had her phone stolen in the street last week.'

'Was she hurt?'

'It was a lad on a bike, he rode past her on the pavement and snatched it from her hand. Sandra tried to hang on to the phone and he shoved her... I said she should have just let him have it, but she said that she hadn't had time to think, it was just instinct.'

'I'm sorry to hear that. Did Sandra fall over?'

'No, but he elbowed her away, and she was a bit dazed afterwards. The police said that we should go to A&E, but she said she felt fine, and she just wanted to go home. I wanted to take her home, to be honest. Did I do the wrong thing?'

The man's voice hitched with emotion.

'I would have wanted to do the same. Take her home, where she's safe.' Lark would have preferred it if her husband had taken Sandra to be checked over, but she could understand why he hadn't. 'Let's concentrate on how she is now. She's been feeling unwell for three days?'

'It started on Friday evening. She took her painkillers and we went to bed, usually that stops the migraine, but she woke up early on Saturday with a thumping headache.'

'And she's been taking her medication since then? How often has she needed it?'

'She's been in so much pain and the pills don't seem to make any difference. I was afraid she'd take too many, and I took them away and only let her have them according to the instructions on the packet.'

'That's good. Really sensible. Stan, I understand how worried you are, but I need you to hold on for a moment, so I can look up my record of having seen Sandra…'

Will had been sorting through the bundles of post, but now he reached for the secure cabinet under the reception desk, unlocking it. He handed Lark her tablet and she called up the notes she'd made when Sandra had come to the clinic.

'You're only ten minutes away from here…'

'Yes. We don't like to make a fuss, but if someone could see Sandra… This doesn't seem right.'

That was often the most telling thing. A

member of a patient's family who knew that something wasn't right shouldn't be ignored.

'I've got a better idea, Stan. You and Sandra sit tight and I'll come to you…'

Will waited for her to end the call, and Lark handed the tablet over to him as she put the phone down.

'It's a patient I saw last week. I gave her some lifestyle advice on how to manage her migraine, and her husband says she's been better, but now she's been incapacitated all weekend.'

'Could be the result of her relaxing after stress.' Will looked up at her. 'You don't think so?'

'It's a possibility. But she had her phone snatched in the street last week. Apparently, she tried to hang onto it and was shoved. And now the headache doesn't seem to be responding to her usual medication…'

'She was seen by someone?'

Lark shook her head. 'She said she felt okay, and that she just wanted to go home. There's a small chance that this isn't a migraine.'

Will nodded. 'Would you like me to come with you?'

That would be good. Will assessed people for possible head and neck injuries every day, and as a doctor he was able to write a prescription if one was needed.

'Maybe I should stay here. Pete said that he'd be emailing a list of suggestions through to us this weekend...' Even as Lark said the words, she realised that she had her priorities upside down.

'So...what? You're going to wait for an email when you could be coming with me to see a patient? I know you're worried—'

'Yes, I am. But you're right, hanging around waiting for emails isn't the way to deal with it,' Lark interrupted him, reaching for her jacket. Hopefully, whoever had last used the charity's electric car, garaged in the basement car park, had remembered to leave it charged up.

CHAPTER THREE

WILL WAS GLAD that he'd decided to come along. When he parked outside the small house on one of the central London housing estates he saw a man open the door. Lark introduced them, and they were shown into a neat sitting room where a woman was lying on the sofa. Stan was hovering, clearly worried about Sandra, and Lark drew him to one side so that Will could examine her.

'I'm so sorry to bring you out...' Sandra was trying to sit up, her head obviously hurting her badly. Will helped her, then knelt down beside her.

'It's no trouble. May I just check your head for any bumps?' It was often difficult to distinguish between the symptoms of a migraine and a concussion or mild traumatic brain injury, and looking for any signs of the head injury itself was a good place to start.

Sandra was bleary-eyed and clearly in a lot

of pain. Will couldn't quite assess what the look on her face meant, but when she touched the side of her head, Lark noticed the action too. She murmured to Stan that maybe they should leave Sandra and Will alone, and Stan offered to make a cup of tea.

Then he realised. Sandra *had* been hurt and she'd been keeping it from Stan. He reached out, gently exploring the side of her head, and found the bump. 'Do you know when this happened? Was it when you had your phone snatched?'

'Yes. Stan was so upset and angry... He'd walked on ahead.'

'Yeah. Blamed himself?' Will could identify with that. If it had happened to Lark, he would have felt just the same.

'Yes. It's stupid, but...' Sandra shrugged miserably.

'No, it's not. We've all been there, Sandra, someone we love is hurt and we're unable to help.' The old agony began to stir in Will's heart. Echoes of when someone *he'd* loved had been hurt. Now wasn't the time to think about that, he had a job to do here. Will repeated the old mantra to himself. He was okay and he could function. He could carry on, the way he'd done for more than ten years, now.

'You didn't tell him?'

'It's probably nothing. I've bumped my head

before now.' Sandra straightened a little, but the effort seemed too much for her and she leaned back onto the sofa cushions.

'Yes, you're right. The overwhelming possibility is that it *is* nothing, and that what you're experiencing is a bad migraine. But I think we need to check, just to be sure. Just knowing may well help you to feel a bit better.'

'Yes. All right.'

'There are a few more tests I'd like to do first. One of them is going to involve shining a light in your eyes, just for a moment. I know that's not what you want right now...'

'It's all right, Doctor. I'll manage.'

Sandra had managed, even though she'd begun to retch when Will had checked the reactions of her pupils to light. Lark came hurrying into the room, holding a roll of kitchen towel, and deftly caught up a disposable vomit bowl from the medical kit they'd brought with them. When he took it from her, she grinned at him and Will reckoned he'd be in for one of Lark's dry comments about doctors not being supposed to take vomit bowls from paramedics, later. Lark had always been more aware of that difference than he was, even if her reaction had turned from looks of quiet suspicion to teasing a long time ago.

'What do you think?' Sandra was leaning against her, her eyes closed, and Lark held her gently. Her ability to calm and reassure people was something she never measured against his qualifications, and Will always felt that was an omission on her part, which wasn't like Lark because her sharp mind usually took in everything.

'She has a bump on her head and a very slight dilation of the pupil, both on the right side, which is the side of the headache. It may be nothing but we need to make sure.'

Lark nodded. 'You want me to call an ambulance?'

He was quite capable of doing that himself. Now wasn't the time to remind her of that. And they were only five minutes from the hospital where Will worked.

'It'll be much quicker and better all round if we take her ourselves. I can phone ahead and speak to someone in Neurology.'

'Yes. Good. I'll go and let Stan know, and explain that we're just being ultra-careful. He didn't mention to me that Sandra had banged her head.'

'It was when her phone was snatched. Sandra didn't think it was anything, and didn't mention it to Stan.'

'Ah, okay.' She nodded. No need to say any

more, he could rely on Lark to break the news gently.

They carried a folding wheelchair in the boot of the car, for just this eventuality, and Lark went to fetch it while Stan came to sit with Sandra. He shook his head in gentle reproach and Sandra managed a smile as Will took out his phone, dialling the number of the neurology department at the hospital.

Lark didn't come to this hospital much, but since the neurology department was a centre of excellence she'd transported a few patients here. From the moment they walked into the building it became apparent that Will was well regarded. He didn't push, but his quiet conversation with the A&E receptionist brought a nurse out to show them through to a cubicle almost immediately, and a young woman doctor appeared as soon as Sandra was settled on the couch.

'Such a fuss...' Sandra whispered to her, blinking in the bright overhead lighting. Lark held her hand up to shade Sandra's face from the glare.

'It's okay, just close your eyes if the light's hurting you. Let them make a fuss if they want to, we want to make sure you're all right.' Lark was becoming more and more convinced that there was cause for concern, and that this wasn't a simple migraine.

She handed her tablet to Will, containing the observations from when she'd first seen Sandra, along with today's notes. He fiddled with it for a moment and then walked over to the nurses' station, plucking a sheet of paper from the printer and handing it over to the doctor. There was a quiet conversation, in which Will appeared to do most of the talking, and then the young woman walked over to Sandra.

'Hi, Sandra, my name's Dr Shireen Madani-Porter and I'm from the neurology department here in the hospital. Dr Bradley's already examined you and I'm afraid I have a few more tests I need to do, now that you're here. I know your head's hurting, so I'll be as quick as I can.'

'Thank you, Doctor,' Stan replied for Sandra, watching as Shireen carefully checked Sandra's responses, noting everything down. Lark motioned him to a seat, sitting down next to him.

When she'd finished, Shireen walked over to Will, who was standing in the corner of the cubicle, watching silently. She proffered her notes, and Will ignored them.

'I'd like to do a CT scan, and keep Sandra in until we can be sure exactly what's going on,'

Shireen murmured and Will gave her one of his brightest smiles.

'Great. Thank you.' He nodded towards Stan, in an indication that Shireen should now tell him what would be happening next, and she hurried over to him, sitting down in the seat that Lark had just vacated for her, and began to talk to him.

It was time to go. Lark squeezed Sandra's hand, smiling at her and reminding her to do as she was told, and then nudged Will out of the cubicle.

'We can't hang around here all day...'

'No.' Will frowned. Something was clearly bugging him.

'What?'

'Nothing. Just...how do you do this? Bringing people into the hospital and just leaving them here. Don't you wonder about what comes next for them?'

'Yes, of course I do. But there's always the next person waiting for me. It's a matter of trust, and knowing I'm handing my patients on to people who will care for them well.'

'Mm. Suppose so. Shireen's very thorough and she's a good doctor. A little new, and she's still finding her feet...' Will looked round as the cubicle door opened behind them, and Shireen appeared. 'Everything okay?'

'Yes, thanks. I'm just going to order the CT scan, and I'll make sure that Sandra's taken up to the ward as soon as possible.'

'Give me a call...'

Shireen's face fell and Lark resisted the temptation to kick Will. 'It would be great to know how Sandra's doing. If you have the time, that is.' She smiled at Shireen.

'Oh. Yes, of course.' Shireen got the message that Will wasn't checking up on her and grinned, hurrying away.

'Really? *Give me a call?*' Lark waited until they were outside, walking back to the car.

'It's a perfectly reasonable request.'

'You're happy that she can manage Sandra's case?'

'Of course. I have absolutely no doubt of that.'

'Then let her do it. Ask tomorrow. Or ask today if you must, but make it clear that you're not questioning her ability, you'd just like to know. Or you could call Stan, he's given me his number and I said I'd give him a call this afternoon.'

'Oh. Now you tell me.' Will feigned outrage. 'So much for your ability to walk away and not look back, then.'

'You're not the only one who's human,' Lark flashed back at him, getting into the car.

***

When they returned to the charity's office, riding up in the lift with the receptionist, they found their morning coffees still standing on the front desk. Grace tutted at them both, sweeping off into the kitchen to empty the cardboard cups, and Will retreated to his office to make some calls while Lark went through Howard's post.

An hour later she popped her head around his office door, holding two more cups of coffee, this time from the machine in the kitchen. Will motioned her inside, holding up one finger to indicate that the call he was making was drawing to a close, and Lark put the coffee down, flopping onto the sofa opposite him.

'I just heard from Stan. He'd gone for a cup of tea while Sandra was having her CT scan. There's no news yet, of course, but just knowing she's being well cared for has made all the difference. He told me that Shireen's been really kind to them and he asked me to thank you as well.'

Lark had regained the warmth, the certainty that he'd seen eroded in the last week, and what he'd been wanting to say to her seemed suddenly very relevant.

'I'm glad to hear it. I've been thinking…'

'Yes?'

'We're medics, and Stan and Sandra are the people we're here for. They're at the centre of everything we do.'

'Of course.' Lark's gaze seemed to consume him.

'Howard's our friend and he's going to need some help and support when he's discharged from rehab.'

'Without a doubt. A stroke of that severity means he's facing a long road to recovery.'

'That's what matters. It's what's always mattered. This business with Pete and the trustees, the fooling with our heads, the competition and changing roles… That's all secondary, and we've been spending too much time and energy on it. That has to stop here.'

'Sure, boss. Whatever you say…'

'Lark, I'm serious about this…'

They stared at each other. Lark's response was no different from the jokes that they shot back and forth at each other all the time. But Will's reaction was different. Maybe because everything around them seemed to be shifting, and he could see Lark anew as the one immovable centre of his life. Maybe because he saw her vulnerability too, and felt so darn protective of her.

It didn't really matter *how* it had happened. It

just had, and now he was falling a little in love with her. Blossoming love required a lighter touch than friendship, a little more reassurance and a little less pretending to ride roughshod over each other, even though they were each in the habit of listening carefully to what the other had to say.

And Lark knew this as well as he did. That a joke had exposed the shift in their relationship.

'Sorry, I didn't mean to be autocratic. I'm just a little stressed about all of this.' Particularly since, in Will's mind, the word love always carried the inevitable addendum *and loss*.

Lark nodded. 'You weren't. I always appreciate it when you don't mince your words, and you're right, this does have to stop. If we don't draw a line under it all, this business with Pete and Sir Terence *is* going to compromise everything we do.'

'Solutions?' He grinned at her.

'They want to make this all about personal development, then we'll play it their way. It happens during our personal time, not at work. We take control of it. We've already got a plan for next weekend.'

'And they say that I have all the good ideas.' He grinned at her. However their relationship might be changing, they were still friends.

Friends, doctors. Those were the two absolutes that they had to hang on to.

They'd spent the afternoon seeing patients, as usual. Will had made a point of suggesting they stay behind after work to review Pete's emailed list of ways they might swap roles, and none of it seemed any fun to him. One of the entries suggested that they swap over who made the tea, and since they usually took turns that seemed a particularly fruitless exercise.

Lark looked up from her laptop, where a copy of the list was displayed, her eyes flashing gold in the evening sunlight that flooded across the room. Her large, impeccably tidy desk dominated the space, the small floral sofa relegated to one corner of the office.

Will leaned back in one of the seats arranged on the other side of the desk, stretching his legs. 'I reckon we can knock half a dozen things off it without even breaking a sweat.'

'Yes. I'm a bit miffed about the tea-making one. I'm going to have to make as much as you do, am I?'

That wasn't Lark's objection to the idea—or his. Will knew that it was the thinking behind it, the assumption that Lark made tea and Will drank it.

'Perhaps we'll have to make a biscuit baking rota.'

The joke had the desired effect and Lark smiled. 'No, I think biscuits are off the table. You know I don't bake.'

'So...since we can tick off half a dozen things from this list pretty much immediately, why don't we concentrate on the weekend? Make it clear to Pete that this is the way we want things to go.'

'Okay. So I'll come to your parents' party with you?'

'I was thinking rather more along the lines of me going with you, actually.'

The idea did seem a little crazy, but every time Will tried to dismiss it, he had a vision of Lark, her hand slipped into the crook of his arm, at the centre of everyone's attention. Shining in public, in the same way he'd seen her shine in private over the last four years. Ever since Friday afternoon, when he'd been so determined to defend her, and Friday evening, when she'd melted into his arms, it had been all he could think about. Will wasn't entirely sure how he could have failed to feel all of this before.

'You're sure about that?' She shot him an unconvinced look.

'Positive. And what did you have in mind—

are you going to get on with that painting you've been talking about?'

'I was thinking I might. Trust me, Will, you don't want to spend your weekend painting my walls.'

'Why *are* you painting, anyway. I thought you and Robyn decorated a few years ago, when you first bought the place.'

'Yes, we did. But we couldn't agree on colours, so we compromised and painted everything cream. Now that I have the place to myself, I think it's time for me to try out a few new colours.'

'Perfect. So you're remaking your space, then.'

'You could call it that if you liked. Actually, I'm going to be working pretty hard and getting paint all over me. Have you ever painted anything before?'

'No.' Will decided that body paint didn't count, and that it was probably best not to mention that right now. 'So I'll give you a heads-up on what we're trying to achieve at the party, and you can show me how you want your room painted.'

Lark was shaking her head slowly and the urge to vault across her desk and silence her questions with a kiss tugged at Will. For a start, he wasn't quite sure he could make that kind of leap without disturbing any of the carefully arranged things on the work surface. Secondly, he wasn't in the habit of silencing women, and in particular not Lark.

'If you think it's too much of a challenge...' The suggestion was sure to make Lark's hackles rise.

'No. I'm just worried about my sitting room,' she flashed back at him, and Will felt something stir in the pit of his stomach.

'I'll follow your instructions to the letter. And we have to do something, Lark. Howard's known Sir Terence for a long time and probably has a good idea about how to keep him in check, but I'm not sure that we ever gave him enough credit for the way he protected us and the rest of the staff from ideas like this one. Maybe this *is* the time for us to reassess the way we do things, not because either of us wants to succeed him, but because the balance has changed.'

Lark's face fell. 'I miss Howard. I really do...'

'Yeah, me too. And we're going to have to manage without him for a while.'

'Do you think...? You've seen more outcomes for stroke patients than I have, Will. He *will* be back, won't he?'

'As a doctor...' Will tried to think about what lay ahead dispassionately. 'Howard has everything to fight for right now. His leg's a great deal stronger, and I'm expecting that when he goes into rehab they'll work on that and get him walking again quite quickly. With the right techniques, it'll be possible to release his hand from the clenched position it's in now, although how much fine control he'll have remains to be seen. As he's left-handed, and the stroke affected his right side, he'll be able to manage better with manual tasks.'

'And the aphasia?'

'It'll take a while and a lot of work. But the thing with aphasia is that there's always a potential for further recovery. Howard's determined and he's not going to give up his life's work without putting up a fight, and that's going to stand him in very good stead. You know this, Lark.'

'Yes, I do. I just wanted to hear you say it. It's different that he's our friend, isn't it?'

'Very different. But, as his friends, our job is to believe in him. That means we do whatever it takes to keep this place running, and in good shape for him to come back to. We have to confront this thing with Sir Terence, not just for ourselves but for Howard too.'

When Lark buried her face in her hands, Will recognised the gesture. She was thinking about it, working it through and weighing everything up in her head. The best thing to do was wait, even if he was tempted to add that, in addition to flexing their own authority, it was a scheme that might just allow them to explore each other a little more deeply. That was a temptation that he ought to resist, because all of his common sense was telling him that they already had the best of each other and daring to ask for more was risky.

'You have overalls?' She looked up at him suddenly.

Will grinned. 'Nope. Maybe you could advise on the best ones to get…'

Lark saw where this was going immediately. 'Oh, no. You don't get a say in the dress, Will. I'm drawing that line.'

Shame. From her smile, Lark was probably expecting him to feign a look of disappointment, and Will had no trouble in making it seem real.

'Okay. Fair enough. You've got to give me credit for trying, though.'

Something in her gaze softened. Molten gold showed in her eyes, and the feeling that the only thing he really needed to do was to hold Lark close flooded through him.

'Ten out of ten, Will.' She opened her drawer, taking out a couple of paint charts. 'You want me to show you what you're up against?'

CHAPTER FOUR

WILL HAD GOT in touch with Pete, asking that they move the Friday afternoon session to either the morning or the evening, because the afternoons were ring-fenced for working with patients. Pete had said that the early evening suited him best, and they'd gone to the session with a renewed sense of determination. Will had subtly taken control of the conversation, telling Pete how useful they'd found some of the concepts behind the exercises, and that it had inspired them to take his ideas a little further. Pete had listened, and then Lark had taken over, outlining their plans for the weekend.

And it had worked. Pete was engaged and interested, and Lark felt much happier with the session and less personally confronted. Will had worked his magic.

Only it wasn't really magic at all. She'd known this all along about Will, but before all of this talk of role-playing Lark had never taken the trouble to quantify it. Will's charm seemed effortless because he was actually making no effort to appear charming. Working with him had taught her that he was a nice guy who genuinely liked people, valued them and listened to them. That was all he was doing with Pete—it was all he ever did.

'You know... I think that Pete has a lot to offer. Some of his ideas could be interesting if they were developed the right way,' Will mused as they walked down the concrete steps to the underground car park beneath the building. The weekend officially started now, and he'd said that they had no time to lose taking buses and trains.

Lark turned the idea over in her head. 'Do you feel that your family underestimates you?' Pete had asked the question, but Will had effortlessly deflected it.

This time he answered. 'My parents have always been entirely supportive of my career—of anything I've ever wanted to do, in fact.'

'They value your charm, though.'

Will shrugged. 'Dad's always said I could get away with almost anything. I don't like to think of myself as that manipulative.'

'I've never thought you manipulative. You're not charming either.'

Those baby-blue eyes. The sincerity in them

added a whole new layer to their jokes and the smiling compliments they paid each other.

'Thank you. That's a really nice thing to say.'

Lark lived on the outskirts of London, and Will spent the whole of the journey basking in the glow of what she'd said to him. Calling him charming *was* dismissive, because it didn't take account of the work he'd done to succeed. In his father's eyes it had all been easy. Will was the charming one of the family, and everyone else had to work for what they had.

It wasn't meant cruelly. His father didn't even mean to be unsupportive. It was just one of those things. Everyone had a role in their family and Will's place was to be charming. To somehow feel less, as a consequence of that. To interact with people and then move on.

That wasn't easy. But after he'd lost Eloise, it was the only way he could find any peace. Will had been an awkward teenager, in love for the first time, and she'd left him lost for words. He'd been clumsy and blushing when they'd first kissed, but Eloise had forgiven him and taught him how to kiss properly, since she had the advantage of being six months older than Will, and thus more knowledgeable about the ways of the world.

The sweet innocence of it all still made him

smile. Eighteen months later, they'd gone to London together, Eloise to study English literature and Will to do his medical degree. They'd traded their virginity with each other, in Eloise's narrow bed in her student lodgings. And Will had known right there and then that she was The One. The Only One. Because what they'd lacked in terms of practical experience they'd made up for with a youthful sense of adventure, which made all of the First Times that they shared so special.

London had been good to them, and Eloise had found work while Will continued his studies. They'd grown from teenage lovers to fledgling professionals who had their lives ahead of them and couldn't imagine spending those lives apart.

And then the unthinkable, a series of chances that had culminated in tragedy. If Eloise hadn't turned to wave him goodbye and wish him a good day, if an impatient driver hadn't been late for work, then maybe she wouldn't have been hit by the car speeding away from the lights. He wouldn't have felt her grip on his arm begin to loosen as he fought to save her, and she wouldn't have died in the road before the ambulance could get to them.

Everyone had been kind. His academic supervisor at the hospital had reviewed Eloise's case with the head of A&E and they'd both assured Will that her injuries were too devastating, and that even the most experienced doctor couldn't have saved her. He'd done the right thing at the end, by simply holding her. He'd been told to take whatever time he needed, and his parents had insisted he stay with them for a while. Will had spent two weeks in a daze, hardly speaking to anyone, and then he'd come back to London.

He'd found that the appearance of happiness was something that could be learned. He'd struggled with sleep, hiding it from everyone, but he'd not been able to hide the migraines that hit him when exhaustion had rendered him unconscious for twelve hours at a time on his days off. On the first anniversary of Eloise's death, Will had promised her that he'd cut back on his gruelling work schedule, and balance his sleep patterns a little better, which had finally lifted the debilitating headaches and sickness.

When he'd started to accept a few more of the invitations that hadn't stopped coming his way, Will had found that concentrating on other people's lives allowed him to forget that he didn't quite believe in the one that he was pretending to live. Piece by piece, year by year, he'd built a new life. One which centred around the present and not the future, and where relationships might come and go as naturally and unremarkably as incoming and outgoing tides, which swept a beach clean and fresh each day.

Lark was the exception to that. She was so different from him that it felt safe to allow her in, past the wall of charm.

Pete had wondered whether Lark was invested in her role as a carer. As she sat quietly in the car next to him, Will wondered whether Pete had attributed the right emotion to the wrong person. Didn't *he* have an investment in Lark's family commitments, because in practical terms they had meant she had little time for a romance…?

And now Will was playing with fire. Spending time with her out of work, changing places with her. Hugging her. So many things that he'd thought about doing and then dismissed as being way beyond the confines of their relationship. But going back now would be like standing on the beach, expecting the oncoming tide to recede at his command.

It was relatively unusual to find a bungalow in the London suburbs, but Lark had done so, in a street that combined several one-storey properties with larger two-storey houses. He drew into the double parking spot next to Lark's car, feeling a need to stretch his limbs after having been cramped with his thoughts. As usual, Lark was out of her seat before he had time to reach the passenger door and open it for her.

She opened the front door, flipping on the lights and motioning him inside. The right-hand side of the property was taken up by an open-plan seating, dining and kitchen area, and Lark had clearly been busy, moving furniture to the centre of the space and covering it with dust sheets.

'It's an ambitious job. You didn't think of calling in a painter and moving out for a couple of days?'

She grinned up at him. 'Are you saying that it's too much for you?'

'No.' Will knew that in the face of one of Lark's challenges the best way forward was to show no fear. 'You might have waited until I got here, so I could give you a hand with the furniture.'

'I suppose I could have. But I was rather looking forward to the sight of you in painting overalls.'

Will wondered whether she could be looking forward to that quite as much as he was looking forward to the dress for tomorrow evening, and decided that wasn't possible.

'I suppose I'd better go and get them from the car, then. Those are your colours?' He pointed towards the tester squares painted on the wall.

Lark nodded. 'Yes, the light pinky-beige is for the dining area and the very dusky pink is for the sitting area at the back. The kitchen's going to be much lighter, I'll do that in a warm white.'

'Nice.' Will nodded, feeling on more solid ground with colour choices. Lark had talked about making the bungalow 'hers' when Robyn had left to get married, and he suspected that the hard work involved was partly an antidote to missing her sister.

'I'm not sure how it's going to look.' Lark regarded him thoughtfully. 'But I suppose if I'm redefining my space that allows me to be a bit adventurous. Would you like some dinner before we begin?'

In for a penny, in for a pound. Suddenly Will couldn't wait to get on with the job.

'Or we could make a start, and order in when we get hungry...'

Eight o'clock on a Friday evening. Will probably didn't usually spend Friday evenings at home, but Lark reckoned that he would be attending to his busy social calendar rather than turning his hand to DIY. All the same, he'd changed into an immaculate set of overalls, clearly purchased specially for the occasion, and they'd made a start on the painting.

'It's very blotchy.' Will was frowning furiously at the paint he'd applied to the dining area end of the wall, and Lark walked across from her section of paint in the seating area.

'That's how it's supposed to be—the paint goes a slightly different colour as it dries. And the first coat is always a bit blotchy, when you do a second it'll be fine.'

'I was thinking it would be better to put it on a bit more thickly.'

'No, don't do that, you'll get an uneven finish. Two thin coats is better than one thick one.'

Will was clearly still unhappy with his efforts. 'Where did you learn to do all this?'

'My dad taught me. It's a life skill, isn't it?'

He shot her an unconvinced look. 'My younger brother always used to help my father with any DIY jobs that needed doing. Edward's the practical one.'

'And your brother Joel is the academic. Which doesn't leave you much ground to occupy, does it.' Lark had never questioned the way Will's family did things, but right now it seemed a pertinent observation. One that Will seemed to be struggling to find an answer to.

'He always says that I'm the *"people person"*.' Will motioned a pair of speech marks in the air.

'So being a doctor doesn't take practicality? Or academic work?'

Will shrugged. 'My thoughts entirely. Families, eh?'

It wasn't much of an answer, but it seemed to be the only one that Will was going to give. And it was accompanied by the look that Will used whenever he was trying to smile his way out of an awkward question.

'So what do you think of DIY then? I find painting quite relaxing.'

He laughed, shaking his head. 'I'm a bit stressed out with it at the moment. Since you've done more than I have.'

Lark glanced at her part of the wall. 'Getting competitive?'

'Isn't that okay, when it's just between us?'

Lark had decided not to admit that she'd been spurred on in her work by comparing the areas they'd both painted. Or that she wasn't unhappy about the fact that her patch of dusky pink was a good deal larger than Will's section of pinky-beige.

'It's not about how much you do, Will. I'll order the pizza and give you a chance to catch up.'

'Ah. If it isn't about how much you do, then why would I need to catch up…?' Will shot her a twinkling smile and started to paint again.

They'd sat in the kitchen, drinking beer and tucking into pizza. Concentrating on painting evenly without leaving too many brushstrokes *had* cleared Will's mind of the worries that the week had brought, and catching up with her—competing—had added a frisson to the task. As he'd leaned back in his chair, taking a sip of beer, he surveyed his work with a satisfaction that he'd thought impossible.

They'd worked on, until it was beyond time for Will to go home.

He returned early the next morning, to find Lark, dressed in the pair of paint-spattered jeans she'd changed into last night, a cup of coffee in her hand. The door to the large front bedroom was wide open, and she'd clearly been surveying the room that had once been Robyn's. An empty space that made Will realise that a hole had been left in Lark's life, which wasn't filled yet.

'Are you going to redecorate this room as well?'

She hesitated. 'I was thinking of it. I might move in there, it's bigger.' When they'd talked about it at work, Robyn's leaving to get married had seemed an abstract idea. Here, seeing the almost tangible space that she'd left, it all felt so much more immediate.

'You miss her, don't you?'

Lark led him into the kitchen and poured him

a cup of coffee, then sat down with him at the kitchen table.

'Of course I do.'

'I mean...*really* miss her.' Will ignored Lark's shrugging smile. It was the one she always gave when she was trying to brush off her own needs, in favour of recognising someone else's.

'I'm really happy for Robyn. She has the life that she wanted, and it's what I always wanted for her too.'

'Of course. No one questions that, but you get to feel something too.' Will wondered why he was suddenly pushing so hard, when he'd already accepted Lark's assertions that she was concentrating on getting on with her life.

She pressed her lips together. 'You know...my parents were always so fearful for Robyn. That was why she came to live with me, she needed to spread her wings and it was virtually impossible to do that at home.'

'And you gave her the opportunity.'

'Yes, but Robyn's always been the adventurous one, and I'm the sensible one. I relied on that to persuade my parents that her coming to live with me was the right thing to do. And Mum used to call me all the time, she was so fearful for Robyn. I felt it was my responsibility to make everything work for her.'

'You never said.' Will was suddenly conscious that they really had moved onto new ground. There were a lot of things he hadn't said either.

'I didn't realise what I was doing. I spent years working out how I could make things go right for her, when Robyn was actually perfectly capable of doing that herself, she just needed a bit of practical help from time to time. The real burden was my own fears, and those of my parents.'

'You've come to see that now?'

'Yes, I have.' Lark smiled suddenly. 'But if you ever tell Robyn that's how I felt, there'll be trouble.'

Will chuckled, liking the idea of sharing a secret with her. 'So you really are reinventing yourself, not just painting a few walls.'

'It's more like finding a part of myself that I lost because I let fear get in my way. But not before breakfast.' She grinned at him. 'Then I reckon I can finish up with a second coat on my side of the wall before it's time to think about getting ready for the party.'

'And it would be a shame if we let a mere party get in the way of painting.' Will was only half joking. Last night, he'd started at the front of the house and Lark at the back, and they'd gradually worked their way towards each other, meeting at the point where the wall had been removed between the two spaces. It would be impossible to allow her to get ahead of him now.

'My thoughts exactly. Maybe the smell of paint will loosen your tongue a bit as well...'

Maybe. But right now Will was in this for the sheer enjoyment of it.

It was just a wall. And paint. If it meant something to Lark, then she really shouldn't have assumed that it would mean the same to Will, and her comment about loosening *his* tongue had been out of order, even if there was a lot more going on behind Will's façade than he ever owned up to. But he hadn't seemed to mind, and apologising might give the slip more importance than it deserved.

And this was a lot more fun than painting on her own. It was clearly the first time Will had done anything like this, but he was a fast learner and his greater height and reach gave him the advantage. It was only the fact that he seemed intent on making his side of the wall perfect that allowed her to keep up with him.

They'd never competed over anything before, and they'd both been adamant that they wouldn't cave in to the trustees and compete with each other now. But laughing together over paint splashes was just one part of the pleasure, and the other part was being the first to reach the square-topped arch between the dining space and the living space.

'If we leave at about five, then we'll get down to my parents' place in time for me to introduce you to the family and show you around a bit.' He'd insisted on keeping working on his side of the wall while Lark went out to the local Chinese restaurant to get a takeaway for lunch.

'I'm relying on you, Will...' Lark's usual strategy at large gatherings of people was to find herself something useful to do and help with that, so that she could avoid the need for small talk. She'd never quite fathomed how Will managed to conjure something interesting to say to complete strangers, seemingly out of thin air.

'You just need to get people talking.' He grinned across the kitchen table at her, reaching for one of the boxes of food. 'Everyone has something to say about themselves.'

She wondered whether this seemed as easy to him as the practical task of painting did to her. Lark dismissed the thought that she'd rather be at home, getting on with the gloss on the skirting boards. Will had risen to his end of the bargain, and she'd rise to hers.

At three o'clock she went to shower and wash her hair, leaving Will to clean the brushes. Clothes and hair were just practical things, arranged to help you fit in with your surroundings, weren't they…?

All the same, her hair and make-up took a little longer than usual, and the red dress she'd bought for the evening reception of Robyn's wedding required a little more scrutiny when she stood in front of the mirror in her bedroom. When she went downstairs her high heels clacked disconcertingly on the tiles of the kitchen floor.

And when Will appeared… She'd seen him in a suit plenty of times before, ready for an evening function. Effortlessly handsome. Charming in a way that didn't seem artificial, but just made it seem as if he was everyone's best friend.

Her heart began to beat faster. Lark couldn't compete with this, and very probably couldn't compete with the other women who would be at the party. And then Will smiled that smile. The one that said that she was the only person in the room—the universe, even—who could draw his attention right now.

'You win.'

She stared at him uncomprehendingly. 'Win?'

Suddenly he was very close. His gaze fixed on her as if even this wasn't close enough. Lark shivered, her hand wandering nervously to her hair, remembering at the last moment not to flatten her curls or push them behind her ears.

'You look stunning. I can't even hope to compete with you tonight, so I'm going to give up gracefully before I make a fool of myself.'

It was a nice thing to say. His words were laced with sincerity, and Lark felt the fluttering of her nerves begin to calm.

'You're making me feel better, aren't you.' Lark still couldn't quite accept the compliment.

Will leaned forward. 'That would be very rash of me. If you were to stop looking so terrified and smile, then I wouldn't be able to take my eyes off you. So while I'm driving, perhaps you could contrive not to feel any better.'

Lark couldn't help laughing. And when Will escorted her out to his car, opening the passenger door to let her get in, and closing it again with a firm sweep of his arm, there was nothing to do but dissolve in the pleasure of his scent, the quiet delight of glancing every now and then at him as he drove. More than an hour later, they drew into the driveway of a large modern house, ablaze with light, in the rolling Hertfordshire countryside.

'Will!' His mother, Priscilla, was looking fabulous as usual, in a blue dress that flattered her curves. As soon as Will stepped inside she enveloped him in a hug. 'And Lark! It's so nice to see you again. I've been hearing a lot about you.'

Will chuckled at the awkwardness of the moment. 'All of it quite unrepeatable.'

'Nonsense, Will.' His mother turned to Lark, holding out her hand. 'He pretends to be such a rogue...'

And, like any mother, Priscilla Bradley saw straight through him. Will's careless charm fooled his mother about as much as it did Lark, and she too ignored it.

The caterers were busy stocking tables at one end of a large high-ceilinged area that was far too grand to be called a sitting room. To one side, a table had been arranged with information about Migraine Community Action's work subtly displayed, so as not to be too intrusive, but there for those who wanted to know more. When Priscilla excused herself, saying that she should go and see what was going on in the kitchen, Will caught Lark's hand, stopping her from following her, and led her through to the back of the house. William Bradley senior was in his study, talking with his son Edward, who motioned to Lark to sit down on the sofa next to him.

It was a nice gesture. Edward shot Lark a quiet smile as his father and older brother went through what was clearly an established routine of challenging each other over who had been the busiest since they'd last seen each other.

Will's father slapped him on the back. 'We have some interesting people here tonight. Your mother added a few to the guest list that you sent, who are all interested in seeing how your charity works.'

'I didn't think she'd be able to resist.'

'Your mother loves a party. She'll be directing the food and drinks operation so that you can get on with talking to people. Ed and I will…' his father waved his hand in the air '…support.'

She heard Edward suppress a snort of laughter. Will and his father were the big personalities in the room, the ones who could hold people's attention, and it seemed that Ed was just as happy to play a supporting role as she was. But Will obviously had other ideas.

'I brought Lark along because it's a great opportunity for her to meet people. You want to join me and Ed in blending into the background, Dad?'

His father's eyebrows shot up in surprise, but then he beamed at Lark. 'Wonderful. Lark, the room's all yours.'

Great. Now she had a whole room full of people to contend with. Will shot her a smile, which was no doubt intended to make her feel she was equal to the task, but for once even Will's smile couldn't penetrate the deep panic that she felt.

CHAPTER FIVE

WILL'S FAMILY WERE welcoming and friendly—but for the first time Lark was noticing how clearly defined their roles were. It sold Will short to imagine him as a charming ambassador when he was so much more than that, and Lark couldn't help wondering if her own attention to detail wasn't inadvertently forcing him into the same role that he had with his family. Maybe she should make an effort to slip into his shoes tonight, and give him some space to show that he was capable of a lot more than just charm.

'What do you think?' Will had extracted her from his father's study, stopping for a moment to exchange hellos with his brother Joel and his wife, who were laughing together in one corner of the empty reception room. Then he'd guided her out onto a covered patio, shimmering with lights and warm enough in the early evening to provide an overflow space from the party.

'I didn't expect your whole family to be here. It's really nice of them all.'

'Yes, it is. They've always been really supportive of whatever I wanted to do.' The corners of Will's mouth turned down for a brief moment and then he smiled, taking her hand and settling it in the crook of his arm in a gesture of intimacy that mirrored the way they worked together. Challenging the hardest issues together, telling each other the truths that would be difficult to hear from anyone else.

'Every family has expectations, Will.' Lark wondered whether the sessions with Pete and the swapping of roles was finally getting to Will.

'Yeah. They all just want the best for me, the way that you want the best for Robyn.'

There was something there. She'd felt it simmering beneath the surface, before it was quickly hidden, so many times and had never had the courage to ask.

'What is it, Will?' She tightened her grip on his arm, as if physical closeness might prompt a greater understanding between them.

'I've told you about Eloise, haven't I?'

'Only that you and she were friends when you were young.' Will had mentioned Eloise once or twice, generally in the context of his schooldays, and Lark had reckoned that they were a little more than just friends from the tenderness on his face. But when she'd asked he'd changed the subject and stubbornly refused to return to it.

'She was my first girlfriend. My first love. We'd been together since we were seventeen. We were going to get married when I finished medical school, but she died in a road accident. I was there, and I couldn't save her...'

His words hit Lark like a blow to the chest. Like every other difficulty in life, Will had skimmed over this tragedy and let everyone think nothing was bothering him. But something like this didn't just go away.

'I'm so sorry, Will.' She felt him shrug and before he could dismiss his own feelings she tugged at his arm to quieten him. 'That's the kind of thing that's never really okay, and you don't get over it. You just learn to live with it.'

'Yeah, you're right. Thanks for saying that.' It was as if a curtain had fallen somewhere behind his eyes, leaving him naked. All Lark could see there was pain and despair, but she couldn't shrink away from that.

'There's more to say, isn't there? Nothing like this simply ends with your parting,' she prompted him.

He nodded. 'Does it sound self-pitying to say that there were times that I wished it had? That I just didn't want to go on without Eloise.'

Will had loved her. *Really* loved her. Lark reproved herself for the jab of envy that she felt. That had never been an issue with any of Will's other relationships—they were all so transient—and she knew that she had the better part of him by being his friend.

'No. It sounds a lot like the reaction of anyone who's lost someone that they really loved. If you have a picture of her that you'd like to show me, I'd love to see it.' If Lark could picture Eloise, then this would all be more real to her and she wouldn't feel so dismayed that Will *had* loved someone. She had no right to feel anything about it at all, other than a sympathetic sorrow over his loss.

He looked around, as if checking that they were alone, and then reached into an inside pocket of his jacket, taking out his wallet and opening a concealed pocket. 'You're not going to tell anyone that I still carry a photo of her, are you?'

'It's not a crime, Will. But no, if you don't want me to mention it to anyone, then of course I won't.'

Will handed her the photograph and Lark caught her breath. 'She's beautiful. You both look really happy together.' The look of open contentment on Will's face made her like Eloise immediately, and Lark could share this reaction honestly with him now.

'Yeah, we were. After she died, Mum and Dad insisted I come back home for a few weeks, and I appreciated that a lot but... I didn't want to talk about it any more. I didn't want people worrying about me either, thinking I was unhappy. So if they asked I'd just say I was fine and change the subject. Get them to talk about themselves.'

Suddenly everything made sense. The way that Will concentrated on whoever he happened to be talking to. The way his relationships never got to the point of being serious, starting and ending without disturbing the pattern of his life.

'So you hid your own pain behind a wall of charm?'

He shrugged. 'I'm not going to deny it, even though it's an uncomfortable thought. I was happier talking about other people and I guess that became a habit.'

'And your family were just happy that you seemed to be getting over Eloise's loss?' It felt a little presumptuous to say her name, but Will smiled suddenly when she did.

'Yeah. This role of mine fitted in with what they wanted for me as well.'

'But you're not comfortable with it now. The way it seems to diminish you.' Lark had been thinking that it ignored Will's very real talents in other directions. But maybe it was his way of rejecting the possibility that he might make a relationship that lasted for more than a few weeks as well.

'I suppose... As you said, all families have expectations. It was a long time ago now, and time heals.' He grinned down at her. 'You paint over the cracks for a while and then suddenly you realise that happiness isn't quite as elusive as you'd thought, and you do actually have a lot to look forward to.'

Maybe that was a veiled hint about Lark's situation. That some day soon she'd step out from behind her own parents' expectations, which she'd so readily shouldered because they fed her own fears.

'So we're going to do this then? I'm going to see whether I can take a leaf out of your book and be the charity's ambassador for the evening?' Lark still felt pretty unequal to the challenge.

He nodded, laughing. 'Trust me. As ambassador in chief, my verdict is that you'll knock them dead.'

Lark had nothing to be nervous about. From the first moment he'd seen her, in a red dress that folded gently around her curves, her beautiful eyes somehow bigger and more lustrous... That wasn't fair. It wasn't the dress or the make-up, and Lark was beautiful any day of the week. The red dress invited Will to look, though, and when he did he felt that he'd discovered something that he'd only half seen before.

All the same, she was nervous. He could almost feel her heart beating faster as her fingers tightened around his arm.

'Over there...' He nodded towards a distinguished-looking man who'd just entered. 'Sir Sidney Chambers. The newspaper guy...'

Lark nodded. 'I've heard of him.'

'And that's Sunil Mehta...'

Lark nodded again. Sunil's generosity, particularly towards medical charities, was well known. Her brow creased and she looked up at Will, clearly wondering what to do with the information.

'We're not here to ask for donations, or newspaper articles, just to introduce you to people so that we're on their radar. Whether they choose to pick up the phone, and when, is up to them.'

'Right. Good.' Lark looked a little relieved. 'Like making friends in the playground.'

Will chuckled. 'Just like that. Remember the newspaper article about different ways to control migraine last year?'

'Oh! I wondered how you'd got involved with

that.' Will had been asked to contribute to a double-page spread, and the hits on their website had gone sky-high for a couple of weeks afterwards. Lark aimed a grateful smile at the back of Sir Sidney's head.

'He gave the reporter who was writing the piece my number, and then stepped back and let her do her job.' It had been a great opportunity for the charity to heighten awareness about some of the issues that lay at the heart of their operation.

'Okay.' Lark smiled up at him. 'I'm getting the drift of this...'

She certainly was. Lark was irresistible, honest, natural and beautiful. Will was barely stopping himself from whisking her off to a quiet corner and talking to her for the whole of the evening. Feeling her gaze warm him...

'Who's that?' She nodded towards a woman that his mother was welcoming, deftly catching up a drink for her from a passing waiter. Lark's finely tuned radar had caught the body language between the two of them, the expressions of warmth on his mother's part in response to a slightly forced smile.

'Maya Green. She's a good friend of my mother's and she's here to meet us. Her son's started to have regular migraines recently, and she's dealing with a lot of anxiety over it.'

Lark nodded and then started forward, towards his mother. Will grinned. She'd made her choice between money, influence and vulnerability, and he couldn't disagree with it. He watched as Lark hovered awkwardly, trying to catch his mother's eye, and willed her the confidence to just walk up to Maya and introduce herself.

But his mother saw her and drew Lark in, making the introductions. Whatever. If it worked, it worked. A practised, tactful gesture from his mother brought a waiter over, and Lark jumped, before taking a drink from his tray. She pulled a face and leaned in towards Maya, making her laugh.

By the time he managed to circulate smoothly over to the group, Maya and Lark were talking intently, and his mother was listening and nodding.

'...and what about *you?*' Lark asked the question that she always asked their patients' caregivers, and Maya turned the corners of her mouth down.

'I'm okay. You're only ever as happy as your unhappiest child...' Maya shrugged off the question.

'I hear that. And Leo's always going to be the one to really focus on, isn't he. But you're the one standing here in front of me.' Lark smiled persuasively and Will's mother nodded in agreement.

'It's hard. I can't help wondering why this has happened, and whether there's some trauma he's dealing with that he won't talk about.' Maya grimaced.

'Of course. Stress is a common trigger for migraine, but so are a lot of other things. Each person has different triggers—has your doctor talked to you about this?'

Maya nodded. 'Briefly. He doesn't have a great deal of time, and he gave me some leaflets and prescribed tablets for when Leo has a migraine. But Leo just breaks the rules all the time—he stays out late, or spends hours in his room playing computer games. He says that if he's going to have to put up with the migraines, he may as well have some fun at other times. He's his own worst enemy sometimes.'

'It's hard for teenagers with migraine, and their parents. They feel as if they're missing out on things and that it's you who's preventing them from doing what they want.'

Maya rolled her eyes. 'Sometimes it feels as if he blames me for the whole thing.'

'That must be very distressing for you. We do run groups for teenagers with migraine, and if Leo can chat with people his own age about it, that might help. Or maybe a talk with one of our outreach workers would be beneficial—sometimes when information comes from someone outside the family it strikes home a little better.'

Maya nodded. 'You're right about that. I sometimes feel that I'm the last person he listens to. Can…can I call you?'

'Of course. I really wish you would, so that we can talk some more.'

Now was the time for Lark to produce one of the charity's cards, that Will had insisted she put into her evening bag, but she'd clearly forgotten all about them. She looked around helplessly, and Will reached into his pocket, but his mother beat him to it, producing a pen and a small notebook from her bag.

'Oh. Thank you. May I just tear one of the pages out…?' Lark looked a little flustered, but she was delightful. She scribbled a number down, giving it to Maya. 'Would it be all right if I took your number? I'd love to call you next week some time, if that's okay.'

'Thank you.' Maya took the notebook and pen, writing down her own number, and Lark took it, putting it into her handbag.

'Oh. Look, I have some of our cards.' She flashed Will an apologetic glance, and he grinned back at her. 'Will made me put them in my bag and I forgot all about them. Take one of these, but don't call the main number—the one I've given you is my mobile.'

Maybe that wasn't quite as smooth as it might have been either, but Lark was incomparable. Charming and effective in a way that Will could only watch and admire, because he never managed to imbue as much of himself in just a smile. Lark caught Maya's hand and squeezed it, before his mother propelled Maya in one direction and he propelled Lark in the other.

'But I want to talk a bit more…' Lark looked behind her, grinning back at Maya.

'That's okay. You've given her your number and you will. If I'm not very much mistaken, my mother's telling Maya right now that she's to be sure to call you.'

'Is she? I suppose that's all right then.' Lark gave him a taste of her scintillating smile. 'Your family… You're like a tag team, it's all quite brilliantly executed.'

Lark would see it like that. Like an intricate plan.

'My parents have been throwing parties like this for ever. It comes naturally.'

'Not to me it doesn't.' Lark was looking around her, her nerves showing again.

'You're doing fine.' Just wonderfully. Beautifully. Lark was actually better at this than he was, because she gave her heart to it. Will wondered how he could ever compete with her and decided that the fun of trying was everything.

'I'll introduce you to Sidney.' He could see that Sir Sidney was temporarily between conversations, and Will ignored Lark's obvious reluctance, guiding her towards him.

Lark's shyness had made the introductions a little less smooth than they might have been, but once she got talking she betrayed her encyclopaedic knowledge and ferocious passion for the charity's work. And she was open and honest about her own experience of childhood migraine, talking about how it had turned out that chocolate was a principal trigger for her. She'd joked about her chagrin when the various friends and relations who'd looked after her during Robyn's frequent stays in hospital had stopped giving her chocolate treats to cheer her up, but noted that the migraines had become far less frequent.

It wasn't difficult for Will to count how many times he'd made things real and personal by adding his own experience to the mix when talking about migraine. Zero was a number that didn't need a great deal of calculation.

Sir Sidney whisked her away from him, taking her to meet a group of people that Will didn't know. That was one-nil to Lark, although he imagined she didn't think of it that way. He didn't either. Will just was busy envying Sir Sidney her company.

'Going well?' His father joined him, handing him a drink.

'Very well. I'm finding myself slightly redundant.' Maybe he should do the obvious and cover the other side of the room from Lark. Maybe even count the number of cards he managed to give out, but that was actually no contest, because Lark had clearly forgotten about the cards in her bag again and she was currently scribbling her number on a napkin.

'Now you know how I feel when you get into the swing of things.'

'Right. Because overshadowing you is such an easy thing to do.' Will grinned at his father, who chuckled affectionately.

'I've always rather felt you get your charm from your mother. Lark's approach is a little different from yours, though. She leads from the heart.'

Will liked the compliment. 'Yes, you're right. She does.' Maybe he should lead from the heart a little more, although a heart that had been broken was a risky thing to expose.

'You and Lark?' His father's expression made the direction of the innocent-sounding question clear.

'Colleagues, Dad. And she's a friend.'

'I never considered that a problem with your mother.'

'Let it go.' Will felt a shudder of discomfort. He and Lark were something more than the transient lovers who crossed his path from time to time.

'Of course.' His father smiled, giving Will the distinct impression that he knew something Will didn't. 'Don't *you* let it go, though.'

'Oh!' Lark had found her way back to him, and Will could have hugged her. 'I think I'm about to have a panic attack.'

'You're doing fine.' Will grabbed her shaking hand, taking her out onto the patio. The cool air was a welcome contrast with the heat of the room.

'That's better.' Lark leaned towards him and he put a protective arm around her shoulder, hoping that they were out of his father's line of sight. 'This is terrifying.'

'You get used to it.'

'I don't think I ever will. You know I'm a lot happier letting you and Howard do this kind of thing.' She pursed her lips. 'I suppose that's the whole point, though. Stepping out of our roles.'

'Don't look at it like an obstacle course that you have to complete.' Will reconsidered the advice. 'Although, truthfully, I wasn't sure where to start with the painting.'

'Is that an Achilles heel I can see through the hole in your sock?' She was smiling now, which was all that Will could possibly ask of her.

'My socks don't have holes in them.'

'That's true...' Lark let out a sigh, walking towards the balustrade that edged the patio. He saw her shiver, and Will took off his jacket, draping it around her shoulders.

'Thank you.' She smiled up at him. 'You're such a perfect gentleman.'

'Hey. Enough with the insults.' He and Lark didn't indulge in those games.

'Just kidding.'

Right now—this moment. It was the time he could have moved a little closer, in an indication that he was about to ask whether he might kiss her. Will turned away from it, leaning against the balustrade and looking back at the lights of the party.

'There's a pen in my inside pocket. Why don't you put it in your bag?'

'Thanks. I had to borrow a pencil from one of the waitresses just now.'

'You have cards...'

'I suppose so. They seem a bit formal, don't they.'

Will gave in to the inevitable. 'Okay, next

time I'll make sure you have a selection of pencils and torn scraps of paper in your bag. Or maybe I'll just ask Mum where she gets those little notebooks of hers.'

'They are rather cute, aren't they.' Lark grinned up at him. 'But I thought I was only going to have to do this once. I'll need a bit of persuasion to do it again.'

'I can charm the birds out of the trees. Hadn't you heard?' Will laughed as Lark looked around furtively and then poked her tongue out at him.

CHAPTER SIX

THEY WENT BACK into the house through the kitchen, where the caterers were busy setting out drinks and canapés on trays, ready for them to be taken through to the guests. Will's mother had come through to make sure that everything was going smoothly and Lark shot her a smile, making for the sink to pour herself a glass of water.

'I'm sure we have sparkling somewhere, Lark,' his mother called out to her and she shook her head.

'Straight from the tap is fine for me, thanks. I think I've already had too many bubbles tonight.' Lark took a gulp of water from her glass. 'It's a wonderful party, Priscilla.'

'You think things are going well?' His mother hurried towards the kitchen door to open it for one of the waiters.

'It's great, Mum, as always. Thank you, we really appreciate it.'

'It's our pleasure, Will. You know that...'

As his mother turned, her feet went out from under her and she fell backwards onto the tiled floor. Lark was closest and as she hurried over, his mother tried to sit up, pulling at the skirts of her dress, which had ridden up as she fell.

'Okay, Priscilla. Just stay down for a moment...' Lark deftly flipped the material down to cover his mother's legs, kneeling down beside her.

But all that Will could see was Lark's dress, bright red and pluming out onto the floor next to his mother. Like the blood that had begun to leak from Eloise's body as her failing heart had pumped it from her veins and onto the tarmac.

He froze.

'Will... Go and get your father. Tell him that your mum's fine, but that she's taken a bit of a tumble.' Lark's voice penetrated his consciousness and he moved automatically, following her instructions. She had everything under control, and Will had no doubt that she would be doing everything to ensure that his mother was all right.

Movement, finding his father and giving him the exact message that Lark had told him to give, brought Will to his senses. By the time he and his father had got back to the kitchen, his mother was sitting up on the floor, with Lark carefully supporting her.

His father squatted down next to her, a gentle smile on his face. 'What's all this, Priss?'

'Don't make a fuss, Bill. Someone must have spilt something on the floor and I slipped on it. I'm fine.'

His father glanced questioningly over towards Lark and she nodded. 'You came down with a bit of a bump though, Priscilla, and you might well have some aches and pains in the morning. It might be an idea to lie down for a while.'

'Hear that, Priss?' His father picked up the high-heeled silver sandals that his mother had been wearing. 'Your heel's broken. I'll go and get your slippers, shall I?'

His mother nodded, clearly not feeling quite as fine as she'd claimed. Lark beckoned to Will and suddenly he knew what to do. Positioning himself carefully, he and Lark gently lifted his mother to her feet and sat her down at the kitchen table.

His father returned with the slippers, and Will saw his parents safely to the top of the stairs. When he returned to the kitchen, the bustle of the caterers had resumed, and Lark was waiting for him.

'She didn't bump her head, and her reflexes

are fine,' she murmured. 'I dare say she'll have some bruises…'

This was no less than he'd expected of Lark. She'd made sure that his mother wasn't badly hurt, and done so kindly and efficiently, even remembering to save his mother's pride by quickly rearranging her dress. He'd worked with her for long enough to be able to trust that she'd done everything that was needed.

'Thanks. I'm—'

She cut his intended apology short, clearly able to second-guess him. 'Seeing her fall like that must have been a shock. You'd only just been talking about Eloise.'

'It's…' Will stopped himself at the last moment from telling her that it was okay.

'It's not okay, Will. You were talking about how unexpected loss had devastated you.'

He looked into her eyes, feeling their golden warmth comfort his fears. Maybe Lark could chase those fears away for long enough to allow him to fall in love. And when that happened, who knew what might be possible?

But for now, he should get on with the task in hand. Tonight—the publicity and the fundraising—was what made the real work they did possible.

'Why don't you go up and sit with your mum?'

'I was going to make her some hot chocolate, and then come back and give you a hand…'

Lark seemed suddenly confident about the roomful of people that her suggestion would force her to face alone. 'I'm on a roll now. I can out party-talk you any day of the week, Will.'

He knew that already. Lost for words, he bent, brushing his lips against her cheek. It was no more than the brief kisses they'd exchanged at Christmas parties and New Year, surrounded by people who were doing the same, but this was scarily different. He felt her whole body jolt, as if the electricity that was passing through him was running in her veins as well.

'Go on then. Make me proud…' He murmured the words in her ear, and then turned to go upstairs.

The last of the guests had left at two in the morning, just as Lark was beginning to wonder how she might cope if everyone who'd said they'd call her, did. Hopefully, they were just party promises. Will had appeared downstairs to bid everyone goodbye, and to reassure them that his mother was perfectly well and sleeping now.

Will showed her to the door of the bedroom that had been earmarked as hers for the night, swinging it open and glancing inside to make sure that her overnight bag had been carried up from the car and placed on the bed. Clearly, if he set foot over the threshold a silent lever might trigger a series of man traps, and the image of her clinging to him as the walls closed in to squash them, or a horde of scorpions swept across the floor towards them made her catch her breath. Maybe scorpions wouldn't be so bad if Will were there to save her.

'If there's anything you need...' He left the sentence unfinished. Perhaps he knew that Lark would rather face any number of poisoned darts launched from hidden crevices than cross the threshold of *his* room tonight.

'Yes. Thanks.'

'I won't wake you in the morning. I dare say we'll all be sleeping in.'

That was wise as well. Who could foresee the dangers the morning might bring, if he found her still in the grip of a dream where beckoning him inside was the solution to a thousand problems?

'That sounds like a plan. Sleep well, Will.'

The slight twitch of his eyebrow told her that Will probably wasn't expecting to sleep any better than she was.

'Yes. You too.' He smiled suddenly, turning away, and Lark escaped into her room, closing the door firmly behind her.

***

The following morning was reassuringly normal. Edward and his wife had stayed overnight too, and the family was gathered around the kitchen table, laughing and talking over a hearty brunch. Priscilla was clearly very stiff after her fall, but the painkillers that Will had given her last night meant that she'd been able to sleep.

Will looked a little tired, but by the time they started out for home, coffee had revived them both. And as soon as they were on the road his mind was onto the next thing on his agenda.

'Skirting boards? I presume that gloss is a whole different ballgame to emulsion.'

'You want to *paint* this afternoon?'

'It would be good to finish off, wouldn't it? If we don't, we'll have to go back to it next weekend.'

That wasn't entirely correct. Lark had been intending to get on with the job on her own this afternoon and during the week.

'You're taking ownership of my walls?'

'Only one of them. At the moment. I may lay claim to the others later.' He shot her a grin. 'Anyway, you may be busy with phone calls today.'

'Today? It's Sunday.'

'Yeah. That's why I put the business cards

in your handbag. They have the office number on them.'

'Will! Why didn't you say? Have you let me do the wrong thing?'

'No, it's up to you to give out whatever number you like. Sometimes I give people my mobile number and sometimes our work number, it depends on the circumstances. I reckoned that you were just taking ownership of my party.'

She had a lot to learn, and maybe Will did too. She nodded at the large bag of leftover party food that Priscilla had presented her with before they'd left.

'Okay. I'll need someone to help me with all of this food, or it'll go to waste. You can do some painting as well, if you like.'

Apparently there was a lot more to changing roles than just an evening's playacting. Will was getting on with the painting, and actually making rather a good job of it, while Lark sat at the kitchen table, talking to the CEO of a local charity that she'd met last night, who was excited at the prospect that they might work together in the areas where their interests overlapped.

'How do *you* do this?' She put her phone down on the table, next to the cup of tea that Will had made while she'd talked, her head swimming with vague ideas, none of which seemed to make any sense to her.

He laid the paintbrush down and came over to sit opposite her. 'First of all, it's tempting to give people firm answers straight away, but you don't have to. It's intentions that matter, not specific answers, so stay with the thought that the prospect of working with them is an exciting one, and that we can hammer out the details when everyone's thought about them.'

'Okay. So I've made a few vague promises. What do I do next?'

'Turn your phone off, so you don't get any interruptions.'

Lark hesitated. Turning her phone off, when Robyn might need her at any time…

In the unlikely event that Robyn needed someone, the first person she'd call was her husband. She picked her phone up and switched it off.

'Now write it all down—start with the name and number, then a quick summary of what they wanted, and whatever thoughts you have on that.' He grinned at her.

Lark recognised that format. She picked up her pen and started to write, while Will went back to the painting.

'Okay, I've done that.'

He put the paintbrush back down. 'You can switch your phone back on again now.'

Lark grinned. 'You've missed a step.' She folded the paper in two and held it out towards him. 'Here you are.'

Will frowned. 'I was hoping you might…'

'Oh, no. I've done my part, and now you get to work out how to implement it all.'

To his credit, Will didn't back off from the challenge, taking his seat again at the kitchen table and reading through what Lark had written.

'You're going to want an itemised set of workable suggestions, aren't you.'

Lark nodded, beginning to enjoy herself. 'You can mutter a bit under your breath, and then roll your eyes first. Then you can read it through again and realise that there are a lot of good ideas here, and it probably is something that we'd like to move forward with.'

'I can manage the muttering.' He grinned at her. 'Where will you be while I'm doing that?'

'Probably making you a cup of tea. Giving you the odd winning smile and telling you that you're wonderful.'

'That's entirely true, Lark.' He shot her a wounded look.

'I don't doubt your sincerity.' Maybe she'd taken the game a little too far. 'I'll just make the tea, and then I have a message from someone else who'd like to talk to me whenever I have a moment.'

'You don't need to do that straight away. It's Sunday, and everyone understands that they'll probably have to wait until Monday before they hear from you. Or if they don't, they should do.'

'That's okay. I'm on a roll now. Why don't you try a bit of painting, while you're framing your response to my notes? Doing something practical does wonders for me.'

Will hadn't taken her up on her suggestion of painting, and had taken off his overalls and cleaned his brush before sitting down at the kitchen table to scribble his own thoughts at the bottom of her written notes, while he tucked into some of the party food they'd brought back with them. After fielding half a dozen calls, Lark had decided that enough was enough, and switched off her phone, so that she could read through Will's ideas.

'A couple of these are really good, we can implement them right out of the box.'

'And some of them need a bit of work, still?'

Lark nodded. Will's notes betrayed some of his trademark blue-sky thinking and some of his suggestions needed a bit of work, but others were intensely practical. And, rereading her own notes, they had a smack of Will's recognition of potential, without providing any solid answers.

'This swapping roles is a bit more complicated than we thought, isn't it.'

He grinned at her. 'Yeah. It's making me appreciate what you do even more.'

'I just couldn't do some of the things you do.' Lark gestured towards the plate of food on the table. 'You want any more?'

Will shook his head, picking up their empty plates to put them in the sink. 'I think you've already proved that you can do anything you want to do. It's just a matter of deciding what that is.'

'And that's the hard part. Everything seems to be pulling us both in a hundred different ways at the moment.'

And then, suddenly, there was one piece of solid ground. One person who saw her as she was, and wouldn't let her down. When she followed him over to the sink, brushing her fingers against his cheek, it was as much of a surprise to Lark as it obviously was to Will. But she could see from his smile, the way his eyes darkened, that it wasn't an unwelcome one.

Then he reached out, laying one hand over hers. She could feel his warmth now. Slowly… excruciatingly, wonderfully slowly, they were moving closer. Each small gesture requiring a response, because they were both crossing boundaries.

'Is this okay?' Will murmured the words against her ear, holding her gently in his arms. When she looked up at him, all she could see was his blue-eyed gaze, devoid of its usual relaxed charm and full of a far more potent longing.

'I'm not sure...' As soon as she said the words he drew back, and Lark shivered as the temperature of the air around her seemed to drop by ten degrees. 'I mean... I'm not sure but I'd like to find out.'

'So would I.' His gaze searched her face, still meltingly tender. 'But my track record does very little to recommend me.'

Lark wouldn't have put it quite so harshly. But that was one part of it. 'I don't want to lose our friendship, Will.'

'Neither do I. And I have no right to ask you to believe me when I tell you that this is different. Whatever relationship we choose to have doesn't come with an expiry date, not for me, anyway.'

'I believe in you, Will.' This made it even harder, because Will had just stripped away her best reason for not getting involved with him. 'But over the last few months, since Robyn got married, I've slowly begun to realise that when I promised my mum and dad that no harm would come to her if she came to live with me, I was taking on all of their worries and over-protectiveness. And at the same time I believed in my heart that she could live her own life and be independent of them, and I knew that was what she wanted.'

'And that must have been harder than I ever imagined it was.' He leaned back against the worktop, sliding his hands into the pockets of his jeans, as if to reassure her that he was keeping them out of harm's way. She could still feel his arms around her.

'It was confusing, I felt as if I was torn in two different directions. I need to find my own ground again, and work out what I want from life.'

'Seems that we both have some work to do...' Will was staring at the floor now.

'Will, I'd...' Lark gulped in a breath, which only made her feel even more light-headed '... I'd like to have you on my side while I'm doing that work. And to be on your side.'

He looked up at her suddenly. 'I'm your friend. I'll always be on your side.'

And that was all he'd ever be if she let this go now. The thought opened up a whole world of regret. Taking all of her courage into her hands, she stepped towards Will, standing on her toes to kiss his cheek.

Their bodies never touched, and Will didn't move. But fire ignited in his eyes, the kind that could suck all of the oxygen from a room.

'Are you telling me that you want to take this slow?'

Right now she wanted to take it the kind of slow that would last all night and maybe even into tomorrow morning, before it burned itself out. That wasn't what he meant, and Lark dismissed the thought as a bad idea.

'Yes. Slow gives us both the chance to work out what we really want. We're both so different...'

'We can be different. And I can do slow.'

She really wished he hadn't said that, because now the craving for his touch was becoming unbearable. She leaned forward, kissing him on the lips, and this time he responded, his fingers light on her cheek as he kissed her back.

'Who knew you'd be such a great kisser?'

She felt his smile against her lips, his hand resting on her back. 'It's not me. I'm thinking it must be you.'

'A joint effort then.' Maybe together they made something that was more than the sum of its parts. Something that Lark might never find with anyone else. That was yet another reason to be cautious. She could so easily lose her heart to Will.

But now, in this moment, she just wanted to kiss him again. And Will's gaze was telling her that it was exactly what he wanted too. She reached for him and he took her in his arms. Lark felt herself shiver in his warmth, feeling the press of his body against hers.

'It's okay. I'm going to go home...'

That was the reassurance she needed. They could do as they wanted now, because there would be an ending. Not a final one, but a pause before they moved ahead. Lark kissed him.

Free. At last they were free to be together. Will's reserve, his barrier of charm, had disappeared and she could feel the trembling of his limbs as passion overwhelmed the fear that he had hidden for so long. The thought that this was who she really was, the woman who was bold enough to love Will and demand that he loved her, made her legs buckle suddenly and she felt his arms tight around her, supporting her. And then, when he kissed her again, she found her strength.

'This is...more than I ever knew I wanted.' Will's defences were down, and in this moment he was hers. Lark wanted more than just this one moment.

'You'll be staying with me, Will? For the

journey?' Just to give him a taste of what that journey would be like, she dropped a kiss onto his mouth.

'You leave me no choice…'

CHAPTER SEVEN

WILL KNEW HOW to draw the line beneath a kiss, and leave it as an exquisite memory. That was all it had been, a kiss, but still they'd gone further than they'd meant to and promised more than their fears allowed. And yet Will had left her in no doubt that he regretted nothing.

It wasn't over for Lark either. The calls and the ideas could wait until Monday, and furious activity, painting and tidying up, carried her through the hours until she flopped into her bed, unable to do any more. But she could still think about Will, and even the feeling that they'd just stepped over a line and were in dangerous territory seemed to add spice to the sweetness of it all.

And in the morning... Will was just as perfect as he'd been in her dreams. He didn't studiously avoid her gaze, or pretend that nothing had happened between them. But this was no one's business but their own, and he knew that work wasn't the place to talk about it.

'You want to swap offices for the morning?' He finished their Monday morning meeting with a joke.

'Why would we do that?'

'You're going to be on the phone, returning calls for a while. I thought maybe you'd want to pace, or lie on the sofa. Your office, though...' He took in her desk with a sweep of his hand. 'Your office reflects your mindset. It has a pervasive aura of order that might jump-start my responses to your ideas.'

'Don't push it, Will. We're trying out a few alterations to our routine, this isn't a personality swap. I didn't wake up this morning and find my brain in your body.' Too soon, maybe, to be talking about waking up to find herself entangled with anything of his. Lark felt herself redden. Those harmless jokes that they threw at each other all the time probably needed to be toned down a bit.

And then his involuntary reaction made everything okay again. A subtle flush tried his cheeks for size, before it realised that embarrassment wasn't something that Will usually did. He twisted his mouth in one of those gorgeous expressions of regret that said so much more than a smile.

'Good point. Very well made.' His eyes flashed with humour and he rose from his seat, leaving her alone in her office to get on with her calls.

All that Will needed to do was be there. It was an unexpected conclusion to come to, for a man who was used to managing his relationships carefully, being a lover and a companion without ever offering commitment or getting too involved. But that was impossible with Lark. His promise to be there for her was binding. Open-ended, uncertain, and yet still everything that he wanted.

And he could be there. He could wait. The thought of doing both of those things was heady and sweet, and so much more than he'd dared hope for.

Work was promising to be easier this week. Dev would be in the office from Tuesday to Thursday, which took a lot of the pressure off Will and Lark, and meant that they could concentrate more on the clinic and the medical research that lay at the heart of their jobs here.

Maya had called yesterday, clearly distressed, and asked whether she might bring Leo to see them. Lark had offered her an appointment at one o'clock, which was, strictly speaking, her lunch hour, and Will had decided to join them.

They walked through to the clinic side of the top floor office space, smiling and joking together.

They'd worked hard to provide an environment here that would be less stressful for people with migraine, carefully lit with warm LED bulbs, well ventilated, and with a water-cooler in the corner of the waiting room. Maya was sitting on the edge of one of the seats, a young man who had to be Leo next to her.

'Maya...' Lark stepped forward. 'It's nice to see you again.'

'It was good of you both to see us so soon.' Leo didn't look too happy, and Maya was clearly under some stress after a long car journey with a reluctant teenager.

'It's our pleasure.' Lark turned to Leo. 'Hi, I'm Lark Foster.'

Maya nudged her son, and he replied with one word. 'Hi.'

Lark ushered Maya and Leo into her consulting room, and Will followed. There was a desk in each of the consulting rooms, but the main space was taken up by a circular table, with comfortable seating, which they both felt emphasised the collaborative nature of the solutions that they usually suggested.

It was difficult to tell whether Leo's silence was because he was sulking or whether he truly wasn't feeling well, and Will decided it was probably a bit of both. Lark caught up one of the clear plastic folders that held all of the leaflets and documentation they needed for new patients, and handed Will the medication sheet.

His questions about the type of migraine that Leo was experiencing, the triggers and the medication that he'd been prescribed, were directed at Leo and largely answered by Maya. Will was forming the impression that he was getting nowhere fast.

'I just need something to make the headaches go away, that's all. The stuff I have from the doctor doesn't work,' Leo interjected suddenly.

'I'm afraid that's not the way it works. The medication your doctor provides doesn't cure the condition, it helps with the symptoms. Do you take your tablets as soon as you feel the first symptoms of a migraine?'

Leo shrugged. 'It depends where I am. Not always.'

'Well, that's very important. And you might also be able to help yourself by making some relatively small amendments to your lifestyle.'

It was already clear that Leo's lifestyle was the root of the problem. Going out late with his friends, and probably having a few drinks, then sleeping late. Missing meals and grabbing something from the fridge when he felt hungry, and leaving his schoolwork until the last minute.

It was pretty much designed to provoke a migraine, and Maya seemed frustrated and helpless in the face of it all.

Lark was sitting quietly, listening. A prickling feeling at the back of Will's neck told him that wasn't going to last. But she confined herself to shaking her head slowly at some of Leo's answers to his questions, and watching Maya's reactions to what was going on.

The final straw came when Leo claimed that using the computer for his schoolwork was the root of the problem. Maya begged to differ, saying that he spent far more time playing computer games in darkened rooms than he ever took with his schoolwork. Will saw the twist of Lark's mouth, and leaned back in his seat. Any moment now...

'Sit up straight, Leo.' Her tone was so compelling that Leo actually obeyed her, prompting a half-smile from Maya. Lark was going in a little more strongly than usual, but it was obvious from their conversation on Saturday night that Maya was in agreement with her tactics.

'Now take a few deep breaths. That'll make you feel a little less hazy, and you're going to need to hear what I'm about to say.'

Leo shot her a truculent look, but took the breaths. What Lark was telling him was absolutely correct. Slow, deep breaths would reduce stress and might make someone with a migraine feel better, but Will suspected that there was more to it than that. As an ambulance paramedic, Lark had a lot of experience with reluctant patients, and she was using it.

'Here's the deal, Leo.' Lark had caught his attention now, and wasn't letting go. 'Either you accept that you have migraine, and you spend one day a week in a darkened room with a thumping headache, which is increasingly going to cramp your style, *or* you try to do something about it. It's up to you.'

'The tablets don't work,' Leo insisted, this time a little more forcefully. That was exactly what Lark wanted. She was trying to engage him, and if that meant he argued with her then so be it.

'No, they don't. Dr Bradley's already told you that they can't prevent a migraine, they can only treat it. We're looking for something that *will* work.'

'Nothing works. And I can't live my life cooped up at home, doing as I'm told. I need to see my friends.' From Maya's grimace this was obviously a point of contention between her and her son.

'Yes, you do. Shame about that, because I dare say you'll be missing quite a bit in future because, from what you say, these migraines are becoming more regular.' There was no note of sympathy in Lark's tone. 'I can show you how to deal with them, but you have to give me two weeks of your time.'

Leo was clearly calculating his options. Finally, he gave the right answer. 'Okay.'

'Right then.' Lark wasn't going to let up on him yet. 'I'm going to make an appointment with you in two weeks. Same time, Maya?'

'Yes, that's fine. Thank you.' Maya smiled at her.

'Here are some diet sheets, sleep schedules and general advice on computer use.' Lark extracted the sheets from the folder, sliding them across the table towards Leo. 'There are also some exercises for you to try out, and a diary where you can note everything down. And there's a folder to put it all in and keep it together. You do this, and I'll want to see each page of the diary signed by your mother, so that I know you haven't been cheating.'

'It's...a lot.' Leo was glancing through the printed sheets.

'Too much for you?' Lark threw out the challenge, her mouth twisting in a smile.

'No. It's not going to work, though.'

'You tell me that when you've tried it.'

It *would* work. If Leo did all that was included in the carefully written information pack, he'd at least start to feel a little more relaxed and less tired from the late nights, and there was a very good chance that his migraines would be less devastating as well. Lark had understood that asking him to do all this for the rest of his life was something that Leo couldn't countenance, but he'd give her two weeks, and in that time she'd be calling Maya regularly and suggesting amendments to the plan, in the expectation that Leo would agree to another two weeks the next time she saw him.

'Okay. Deal?' Lark reached across the table, holding out her hand. It was a bit theatrical, but Leo's hesitation before he shook on the deal showed that he knew that this was binding.

Lark got to her feet. 'You're interested in computer games, yes? How about I show you how to set things up to improve that environment?' The light room had been designed to show how lighting could be altered to help with light-sensitive migraines, and patients were encouraged to experiment in there. Lark was giving Leo something practical to do, that he could take charge of, and he'd had to earn that concession.

Leo followed Lark from the room, and Maya hung back, smiling at Will. 'Lark was talking to me on Saturday about putting Leo's wellness into his own hands. She's a wonder...'

Will nodded. 'Yes, she is.' More than Maya could ever know.

The waiting room was still empty and there was time to accompany Maya to the light room, where Lark and Leo were messing around with lamps and the computer that stood in the corner, adjusting the seat so that Leo could sit up straight. Somewhere in the process the two of them started to laugh together, and Maya began to relax a little and smile. When they left, there was a marked difference in Leo's attitude.

Will walked back to Lark's consulting room with her. 'Nice one.'

She grinned at him. 'Talking to Maya on her own helped. Migraine's so difficult for teenagers.'

She'd written about that. The swings and roundabouts that everyone went through in their teenage years didn't help when dealing with migraine. But she'd got Leo on her side now, and that was the first and biggest step.

He'd seen this before, a hundred times. He could be authoritative about the medical steps that needed to be taken, and many people reacted well to that. Lark had a way of getting alongside people, an authentic charm which others reacted to. And somehow Will's own reaction was seeping seamlessly from his head into his heart.

'I love it when you're firm.' The words slipped out before he could stop them.

Lark looked up at him, a surprised grin on her face. 'You do?'

All of the ways that she might be firm with him, and all the ways he might be firm back, were hanging in the air between them. Will froze, afraid that any movement on his part might turn into a kiss. Not here. Not now...

'Wednesday evening? Come to dinner, dress code casual, no implications.' It wasn't unusual for them to meet mid-week, to catch up on anything that needed their immediate attention.

'I'll bring my laptop?'

Will shrugged. 'You could. I'd be crushed if you did.'

'You'll cook? At your place?' Lark raised her eyebrows. They'd eaten together numerous times, but cooking was something that Will had always felt might veer a little too close to seduction. His place had been off-limits as well, for the same unspoken reason.

'Wait and see.' It was a little early in their relationship for cooking, but it was the closest thing to making love that Will could think of right now.

He *was* going to kiss her. He couldn't help it.

Suddenly the buzzer in his pocket started to

vibrate and Lark's hand moved to the pocket of her trousers, as hers clearly did the same.

'I'll hold that thought. Patients...' He saw her lips part, as if a full waiting room might be ignored for just a few moments. And then she turned, walking out to greet her next patient.

Wednesday couldn't come around quickly enough. And, by chance, Lark saw Will a great deal earlier than they'd arranged. A patient with a traumatic head injury after a car accident meant that she and her ambulance partner were heading straight for the London hospital where Will worked, which was better equipped to deal with these cases than their local hospital.

She'd worked hard to keep their patient stable during the journey, and it was a relief when the ambulance drew up outside A&E. She and her partner, Alex, carefully transferred their patient out of the ambulance, wheeling him straight through to the rapid assessment centre, where someone from Neurology would be already waiting for them.

'Status?' Will stepped forward, his gaze already assessing the man on the trolley.

'Probable skull fracture, bruising to the right eye and behind his ear—' Lark rapped out her observations a little more concisely than usual, knowing that Will would understand the procedures she'd already undertaken '—he's been slipping in and out of consciousness, and he's becoming increasingly non-responsive.'

'Okay. I don't have anyone to help with him yet...'

'That's okay, I'll stay.' Lark followed him into the cubicle, beckoning to Alex, and they both helped move their patient off the ambulance trolley.

Will's focus was concentrated on examining their patient's head wound, and Lark took off her jacket, pulling on a fresh pair of gloves before she attached the heart and blood pressure monitor to the man's finger. She heard Alex clear his throat behind her, obviously surprised that they weren't already on their way, and she glanced back at him, mouthing that she'd explain later.

'I don't have his name. He was jogging and didn't have anything on him, and no one who saw the accident knew him.' Lark anticipated Will's next question, ducking out of the way as their patient's suddenly flailing arm almost hit her straight in the face. Will caught the man's wrist, gently placing it back by his side.

'He's been doing that a lot?'

'Only once, but he's becoming more restive.'

Will's gaze flipped to the BP monitor and then back again to Lark. A split second of warmth, the sudden recognition that he was glad she was there, and then his concentration was all for their patient again.

'IV fluids and we'll try a mild sedative...' Lark knew exactly what was needed, and focused on finding a vein, while Will rapped out the exact dosage of the sedative.

'Thanks.' Another doctor and a nurse had entered the cubicle now, and it was time for her to step back. Will only had time for that one word, but somehow he made it mean everything—the professional trust and respect between them, and all the other things that she was beginning to feel for Will as well.

'Later...' She whispered the word, wondering whether he'd heard. But now wasn't the time. She pushed Alex out of the cubicle, walking back to the ambulance with him, steeling herself for the inevitable questions.

'You *know* him?' Alex waited for her to stow the ambulance gurney back into the vehicle, and then climb forward into the seat next to him.

'Yes, I work with Will two days a week, at Migraine Community Action.'

'That explains it. Nice to see a consultant who actually realises we're medically trained.'

Lark nodded, and Alex started to manoeuvre the ambulance out of its parking bay. That hadn't been too difficult...

'Gorgeous man.' Alex hadn't finished yet. 'I don't suppose you happen to know...?'

'He's not gay, Alex. Anyway, I thought that you and Jon were back together again.'

'Yes, we are. The rule is that we can look but we don't touch.'

Fair enough. Lark had adopted the same policy with Will, up until very recently.

'What about you?' Alex turned out of the hospital entrance, his mind still on exploring options. 'Is he available?'

'No, I don't think so.' Lark decided not to mention that Will wasn't available because he'd kissed *her* and made a promise to wait. That was all too new to put into words just yet.

'Shame. You could do with a really nice guy, Lark.'

Lark laughed. Will would keep his promises, and she'd be seeing him tonight.

'What, someone that you and Jon can look at but not touch?'

Alex chuckled. 'We won't even look. We'll just make extensive enquiries, to make sure he's good enough for you, and then send you both off to a deserted beach on an expenses-paid holiday. Then we'll enjoy seeing the smile on your face when you get back.'

That would be really nice. Going away with Will somewhere, away from Sir Terence and the constant juggling to keep everything afloat. Away from the nagging thought that losing herself in Will, the man she'd always thought was out of reach, was just another version of losing herself in her parents' unrelenting worries for Robyn. Just Will, and the opportunity to take things slow and work it all out between them.

'That sounds wonderful. I'll let you know when I find the really nice guy.' Lark decided to change the subject. 'What about you and Jon? Any deserted beaches in your future?'

'Yeah, we're thinking about it. We've both got some leave saved, and it would be nice.'

'Do it. You know I've always thought you're made for each other, and you should take your opportunities while you can…'

Will had left work a little later than he'd hoped he would, and rushed home, calling Lark to say that he was delayed, and finding that she too was unexpectedly working late. His cleaner had taken in the food delivery he'd ordered earlier in the day, as promised, and stacked it neatly in the fridge, leaving a note to say that everything was there and thanking him for the chocolate truffles.

He'd been glad to see Lark when she'd turned up in A&E with the patient he'd been waiting for. Even more glad that he didn't feel that he now had to apologise for ignoring her when she and her partner melted away. It was one thing he had in common with Lark that he didn't usually share with his women friends. The demands of his job were usually a stumbling block in their eyes, something that meant that a relationship might be sweet, but it would never work in the long-term.

Will went to shower and get changed, and then got to work in the kitchen. He'd noticed that Lark's fridge was well stocked with good food, but that most of it was easy to prepare, just a matter of finding a suitably sized dish to tip it into then putting it into the oven. He was using ingredients that you had to prepare and mix together before cooking, and he was confident enough in his skill as a cook to know that Lark would be able to tell the difference.

The doorbell rang, and he found Lark outside in the hallway, wearing a pair of cargo pants and sneakers, with a hoodie.

'Sorry... I didn't have time to go home and change.'

The gold in her hair and eyes outshone anything she could possibly wear.

'You look wonderful. I asked *you* for dinner, not your clothes.'

Lark laughed, stepping inside. 'How's our patient?'

'We got a head start on things, thanks to you, and he was operated on this afternoon. He's in Intensive Care at the moment, and we'll need to wait to find out how much he's been compromised by the injury, but I'm optimistic. Oh, and his name was Jack. One of the social workers liaised with the police and they tracked him down and notified his family.'

'Great. Thanks, I'm glad I finally know his name.'

Will ushered her along the hallway and into the sitting room. She looked around and he wondered whether she liked what she saw, in an unusual flash of self-doubt.

'What's cooking? Something smells wonderful.'

'Wait and see.'

'What? You're not going to let me go into the kitchen to take a look?' Lark raised her eyebrows.

'No. If you want to have a look around, the seduction cave is further down the hallway.'

For a moment she took the statement at face value. 'Sorry. You're joking, aren't you.'

'Yeah. It's not down the hallway at all, there's a secret door.'

Will chuckled as Lark rolled her eyes. The slight awkwardness between them, trying to find their feet in a new phase of their relationship, was gone now. This was more like the friendship that they were both so committed to keeping.

'Okay, good to know. I should warn you that it's been a long day and I'm really hungry...'

'Dinner won't be long.' Will took the hint and left her in the sitting room, while he made for the kitchen.

Lark's nervousness about the evening had grown as it became increasingly obvious that she was going to be late. She'd splashed out on a taxi, and by the time it drew up outside the large, solid block of flats in Muswell Hill, she was beginning to feel as if this might just be a mistake.

She'd always wondered what Will's flat was like, and from the outside it seemed nice. The block overlooked the sloping green parklands that led up to Alexandra Palace, and on the other side it was just a stone's throw from a still bustling street of shops.

She'd taken the lift up to the top floor, telling herself that she'd said she was on her way now, and it was too late to back out. When Will had answered the door, the sight of him in jeans and a thin sweater, accessorised with a smile, began to banish all her fears.

And then the jokes and their easy friendship had taken over. When Will disappeared back into the kitchen she was already relaxed enough to take in her surroundings.

The place looked a lot more homely than she'd expected from Will's man-about-town persona. His office had prepared her for the presence of a large, long sofa in front of the open hearth, and Lark wasn't surprised to find that it was very comfortable. But his talent for colour was used to different effect here. Books, plants and the blues and greens of the fabrics gave an atmosphere that was relaxed and soothing.

A heavy oak dining table and chairs stood at the far end of the room, next to the kitchen door. Lark jumped as it swung open.

'Medium well, for your steak?'

Lark nodded. He knew that she liked her steak with just a hint of pink at the centre, and she knew that his would be medium rare. And yet she hadn't even known that Will cooked, although from the aroma that was emanating from the kitchen, he not only cooked but did it well. There was a whole side of him who was a stranger to her.

'You like plants...?' He had none in his

office, and Lark nodded towards the three colourful amaryllis blooms that stood on an oak sideboard, in the light of the window. On the other side of the bay was a large ficus, its shiny leaves and exuberant growth evidencing long-term, loving care.

'My cleaner does, she takes care of them.' He grinned.

Maybe this was all a comfortable pretence, created by someone else. Not Will at all. Lark couldn't help feeling disappointed that even his home kept friends and family at arm's length.

'Your cleaner takes care of everything?'

'Everything that you can forget to water. Anything that doesn't need watering is my choice.' He shot her a mystified look. 'Check out the books if you're in any doubt. Josie has no interest at all in medical titles.'

'That's reassuring. And you haven't got a chef in the kitchen, who'll escape through the window when dinner's ready?'

He chuckled. 'Yeah, a chef that enjoys mountaineering, since I'm on the top floor. Whatever made you think that I wouldn't enjoy cooking?'

'I suppose we don't really know each other as well as we think, do we?'

'I guess not. But I'm looking forward to rectifying that.' He looked over his shoulder at the open door to the kitchen. 'Sorry... I've got to attend to the sauce...'

'Make me proud,' Lark called after him.

Will stopped to take a breath and calm his nerves before he carried the plates through to the dining table, which was crazy because this was a simple recipe that he'd cooked a thousand times. But the steak had left the pan perfect, he was pleased with the way that the peppercorn sauce had gone, and the dauphinois potatoes and vegetables... It was tough to mess up a dauphinois or the steaming of vegetables.

But Lark made every second of those nerves worth it. She actually closed her eyes at one point, as if food was all about savouring flavour and not just something that you needed in order to live.

'This is gorgeous, Will. If I'd known you could cook like this, I would have come sooner.'

If he'd known that Lark would come sooner, then maybe he would have *told* her that he could cook like this. He could have made a regular thing of asking her and Robyn round for dinner, maybe broken down the barriers a bit, so that all of this wasn't such a surprise. But that wouldn't have happened, because Will had kept his distance from Lark the way that he kept his distance from everyone.

'I would have gone to your place sooner, if I'd known too.'

Lark's fork hung in the air as she stared at him. The idea that he was a bit more interesting than the steak he'd just cooked was...gratifying. Will wasn't in the habit of reducing himself to a secondary importance to the things that he hid behind, but it occurred to him that the act of hiding might say a bit more about him than he'd thought. It might say everything about him...

'I suppose that we've always made a habit of keeping our work and home lives separate. I've always been rushing off home for Robyn... But the thing is, I never really needed to. Most of the time I'd get home after her, and find her cooking the dinner.' Lark grinned at him. 'Actually cooking, that is. Not just heating things up.'

Will shrugged. 'Everyone's different. Are you giving yourself a hard time over this?' It increasingly seemed that Lark was.

'I suppose... I regret things. Robyn and I used to have such a great time together, and I was so happy for her when she met Matt.'

'And that's something to regret?'

'No. The opposite.' She took another slice of her steak, leaving him mystified, and Will had to wait for a moment while she savoured it.

'I was so weighed down with the promises I'd made to my parents, and the responsibility that

I felt. I missed out on what should have been a great time, just me and Robyn making our way in the world and having fun.'

'You *did* have fun together, though.' Will had seen that for himself, when Robyn had been volunteering with the charity. 'There were times when I felt I'd never have fun again, after Eloise died, but I came to terms with it, and I can honestly say that I have a good life. We've both had things to work through, and that's okay, isn't it?'

Lark smiled. 'You make it sound okay. I still feel a bit of a fraud...'

'Don't. The fact is that Robyn *would* have found it difficult to come to a new place, find somewhere to live that was suitable for wheelchair use, and make the most of her years at art school and in a new job. You were there for her, and that's what really matters...' Will felt almost breathless, wanting so badly to lift the burden that Lark seemed to carry with her.

'Thank you.' Her eyes flashed gold suddenly. 'So we're both making a new start, then?'

'Yeah. And I'm just grateful that I have your company in that, because I'm not sure I could do it alone.'

'Me neither.'

She gifted him with a luminous smile before turning her attention back to the plate in front of her. It was always nice when someone enjoyed the food he'd made for them, and Will started to eat again, feeling the quiet enjoyment of having done something to please Lark.

'Do you suppose… Everything seems to be so uncertain at the moment, with so much change. Maybe that's not all bad, and it's a chance to remake things, better than they were before.'

Will hoped so. He wanted so much to find that he and Lark could be together, but if she needed to find her way on her own, then he'd let her go. Finish this before it had even started, which was a record even for him.

'What do you need, Lark?'

'Afters? I can't wait to see what you've whipped up for dessert,' she joked, and Will frowned. He'd perfected the fine art of throwing people off the scent, and Lark really shouldn't try it with him, because he saw right through her.

'Besides that.' He smirked at her, not moving from his seat in an indication that he wasn't whipping anything up until she answered the question properly.

'This. I need this. Someone to question me and force me to think about the way I do things. Because I don't have the answers to those questions right now, and I want to find them.'

'Pete, you mean?' Disappointment curled around his desire, smothering it.

'No. Not Pete. He doesn't know us at all, and... That may be his aim, but I'm not sure that he's really hitting the mark.' She shrugged awkwardly. 'You asked me what I needed...'

And she'd answered. Lark might not be able to say that she needed him, any more than Will could admit how much he needed her, but there were only three people who were talking about change, everyone else seemed to assume that things were going on just as they always had. When Pete was ruled out, it was the simplest of all equations. One and one made two. And Will knew that Lark would be there for him, just as certainly as he knew that he'd be there for her.

'Asked and answered, then.'

She nodded. 'Does that mean I'm going to get my dessert now?'

Will chuckled, finding that getting to his feet wasn't quite so impossible as it had been moments ago. 'I won't be long. Stay right there...'

'You're not going to let me watch?' She put on an expression of mock pleading.

'Next time. When I've got to know you a bit better...'

CHAPTER EIGHT

CREPES. EASY TO make and they were a neutral canvas that could be tailored to anyone's precise likes and dislikes. Strawberries were always a good option, or something with chocolate sauce, although the latter was out because Lark never ate chocolate. After some thought, Will had decided that two different options would double his chances of success. Cooking was all about knowing who you were cooking for and catering to their tastes, and he reckoned that getting the reaction he wanted from Lark required either crushed raspberries with cream, or sautéed apples with caramel.

He ignored the fact that usually the reaction he wanted was a kiss. A lot more sometimes. Crepes might be an invaluable aid to seduction, but that didn't mean that they couldn't be used to delight a friend as well.

He made up a plate for Lark, topping one crepe with raspberry coulis and the other with caramel sauce, with a dusting of confectioners' sugar for both. Loading a tray with both fillings, and a stack of crepes so that he could make his up at the table and there would be enough for second helpings, he walked through from the kitchen.

'Oh! They're beautiful, Will!' Lark stared at her plate.

'Don't wait for me. They're best eaten straight away.' He tried not to look as she picked up her dessert knife and fork, cutting a neat sliver of the apple crepe. Will had anticipated she might try the raspberry one first and tried not to stare.

'Mmm. This is delicious.' Lark gave her verdict on the apple crepe and turned to the raspberry one. 'More delicious. That one's totally divine.'

Delicious. Divine. They weren't words that Lark used a great deal in the office, but they suited her, slipping from her lips so easily. Will opened his mouth, about to give some clumsy answer, and she shushed him with a wave of her fork.

'I can't talk and eat these at the same time.'

Silence. Let the food do your talking for you. That was the best compliment that any cook could ask for. Will smiled, reaching for the pile of spare crepes.

Lark emptied her plate and leaned back in her chair, smiling.

'Help yourself to more.'

'I don't think I could.' Lark pursed her lips, clearly reconsidering. 'Actually, perhaps I could manage another raspberry one...'

Raspberries and cream. Sweet with a tart aftertaste. Will mentally filed the information away for next time, wondering if they might explore the full gamut of fillings together. It was a new idea, since generally his relationships didn't last long enough to work his way from apples to... Will pondered on what might begin with a 'z' and settled for 'y'. Apples to yellow passion fruit.

Lark helped herself to another raspberry crepe, and then decided on one more apple and caramel, saying that she badly needed to check whether she really did prefer the raspberry or not. Then she leant back in her seat with an air of finality.

'You didn't buy these, did you?' She turned down the corners of her mouth.

'They're really easy to make. You just need to get the right pan and heat it up properly. You want me to show you?'

'Absolutely. I'm not going to miss out on the chance of having a nose around in your kitchen.' She shot him a mischievous look.

'After we've had coffee.'

'I was wondering if you had coffee in your repertoire. Gives people a chance to talk.'

'I talk...' Will got to his feet, stacking the empty plates. This time Lark got the message that she was supposed to stay put, and let him take them through to the kitchen alone. The idea of letting his food do the talking had just taken on a new angle, and he could think about that while he was making the coffee.

He'd got used to approaching any relationship as a matter of delight. Nice places, great food and then really good sex. None of those things gave a lot of time for talking, or even for thinking all that much. Sight, taste and touch were all about the senses, what lay on the surface rather than in his heart. The fact that what he most wanted to do with Lark was to talk with her banished his doubts. This relationship *was* different.

He finished stacking the dishwasher while the coffee brewed, and then took it through. Lark had collected up the place mats and folded the tablecloth, and was sitting on the long sofa. He noticed that she'd taken off her sneakers, so that she could tuck her legs up onto the cushions.

And they *did* talk. Telling each other stories about when they were children, about growing up and going to university. What had happened before the things which had changed them both, into people who had to think long and hard before they took this relationship forward.

Lark had told him how difficult it had been to convince her parents that she could give Robyn the support she needed in London. How they'd insisted on visiting every weekend at first, inspecting her home and grilling them both on what they'd been doing. And how, even though she was a paramedic, she'd doubted herself sometimes, but that in the end she'd known that she had to support Robyn in reaching out and taking what she wanted from life herself.

How Lark had lost something of herself, that she wanted back now. In the same way that Will had lost something, that he knew he could never get back, when Eloise had died. But Lark had pointed out to him that while he could never get Eloise back, the parts of himself that had loved her were still there, and within reach. No one had ever had the courage to say that to him before, it was too challenging. Far too truthful as well, and much too helpful for a man who needed to move forward.

'It's getting late. We'll have to take a rain check on the cooking lessons and do it another time.' Will was sprawled on the sofa next to her, his feet up on the coffee table.

Lark looked at her watch, turning the corners

of her mouth down. 'I lost track of the time. I'd better call a taxi…'

'I'll take you.' Will gave her a stern look when she opened her mouth to protest, pulling his shoes back on and collecting his car keys from the mantelpiece.

'Okay. Thanks.'

She was silent during the fifteen-minute drive. Quiet moments of togetherness, that didn't require the excuse of food or anything else, but just came naturally. When he drew up outside her one-storey house, she collected her bag from the footwell, and then didn't move to get out of the car.

'It's been a lovely evening, Will. Thank you.'

'My pleasure. I enjoyed it too.'

Silence again. Neither of them moved, as if they were both waiting for the one thing that Will wanted to do. That he felt confident in doing now, because here the pleasure of a kiss couldn't escalate into something that they might not be ready for.

Lark began to fidget, laying her hand on the door lever, as if that was what she knew she ought to do. Will took his courage in both hands.

'May I kiss you?'

She smiled suddenly. 'Yes. That would be nice.'

He was hoping that *nice* was a deliberate understatement. Will used all of his self-control, pausing before his lips quite met hers. Hoping that she could see everything that he felt in his gaze, feel it from the brush of his fingers on her cheek.

And then he felt her hand on his shoulder. Not pulling him in, just gently exploring the contours of each muscle, which instinctively tensed at her touch. Will kissed her, letting the molten heat of her golden eyes flow through his veins.

Exquisite. The raging longing seemed even sweeter because he knew that it couldn't be slaked by this one kiss. Not this one or the next. He could stay here for hours, just exploring the softness of her lips.

He was sure that it wasn't hours, but it seemed like an eternity before she drew back from him. Wide-eyed, her cheeks flushed with things that were unsaid, but could never be undone.

'I'd better go.'

'Yeah.' As soon as Will agreed to the proposition, she was out of the car, bending down to graze her knuckles against the window, and Will reached for the control to wind it down.

'Goodnight, Will.'

'Goodnight. Sleep well.'

She gave him a bright smile, as if she would be sleeping with the same sensation that they were still close, that Will reckoned he would. And then she turned, hurrying to her front door. It was acceptable, required even, to watch her safely inside, and she turned to wave to him before closing the door.

He should go now. As Will started the car, he saw the lights flip on in the room to the right of the porch and Lark appeared at the window, drawing the curtains of the empty bedroom at the front of the house. Maybe they were both moving towards filling the empty spaces in their lives. Will drove away into the night, taking with him the feeling of her lips on his.

A kiss. What could just one kiss in the front seat of Will's car hold? Lark was beginning to suspect that the answer to that was *everything*.

Why else could she have gone to work on the following Friday with such a wildly beating heart? Why would she have to reconsider the smile that sprang to her lips when she first saw him, and then relax again when he shot her a look that told her he had the same impulse she felt? Wanting to greet her in a way that would be entirely inappropriate at work.

And why would she jump every time she heard a knock at her office door? But when Will leaned into the room, still holding on to the door handle, he clearly hadn't come just for the pleasure of seeing her.

'Pete's just had a cancellation and wants to come this morning instead of this evening. How are you fixed for that?'

'I can do that. But we were going to carve out some preparatory time at lunch, weren't we?'

Will shrugged. 'We could improvise.'

'I suppose so. Will you take the lead, Will, just so we're not both going in different directions?'

'It's easy enough. Painting and cooking are off-limits, they're our business.' He gave her a delicious smile, and Lark's heart jumped suddenly. They meant as much to him as they did to her. 'The party's okay to talk about, that was a work event.'

'Okay. Call him back and say this morning's fine.'

Twenty minutes later, when Will ushered Pete into his office and flipped the *Do Not Disturb* sign on the door, Lark was feeling confident that this week would be better than last Friday. Pete had listened to Will's description of how they'd mapped out each other's roles at the party, and swapped them, and had seemed impressed that their enthusiasm for the idea of role-swapping had extended so far beyond the items on the list he'd sent.

'I've learned quite a bit about Lark. And myself...' Will finished up with a smile.

'Me too. What Will does at these outreach events isn't just a matter of natural ability, there's quite a bit of work and organisation involved as well.'

Will nodded. 'I think we're finding that we're not quite as different as we thought. Or at least that we're both able to use our own skills to get the same results, even if our methods might be a little different.'

'And this affects your decisions at work?' Pete asked.

Lark could answer this one. 'I think it widens our options. We're both learning that there's no right or wrong way to do something—what works, works and what doesn't, doesn't.'

'Yeah. Well put.'

Pete nodded again. 'You both seem in agreement about all of this.'

'Yes, I think we are. That's the way Will and I work. We don't agree about everything, but we do discuss things and come to a conclusion that we're both comfortable with.'

'So...' Pete paused for a moment, as if he wanted to alert them both to the fact that they should be thinking about that last statement. Lark glanced at Will, and he shook his head imperceptibly. Talking about things was what they did and surely there was nothing wrong in that.

'Who actually makes those decisions? Comes to the conclusions?'

'It's fifty-fifty. Sometimes I do and sometimes it's Will.'

Will nodded. 'I'd agree with that. Fifty-fifty. There are some issues where Lark has a great deal more experience than I do, and I recognise her greater expertise and let her decide—'

'You *let* her decide?' Pete pounced on the word.

'There are other issues where I've got more experience than Lark, and then she lets me decide. The whole point I wanted to make is that working together as we do, and very much at the same level, requires consensus and a willingness on both sides to acknowledge the other's strengths.'

There was a note of irritation in Will's voice, which Lark shared. The idea that Pete expected him to take the lead in any of their decisions was completely misguided, and an insult to both of them.

'You'd agree with that, Lark?' Pete seemed keen on pushing the point.

'Why would you assume that I'd expect anything different from an entirely equal relationship between two people on the same level at work?' She jutted her chin confrontationally. If Pete wanted to insinuate that she did as Will told her because she was the woman of the team, then he was going to have to come out and say it.

'That sounds like the kind of thing you feel you ought to say,' Pete shot back at her.

'So... Let me get this right...' When Will felt strongly about something, his tone became even more measured and affable than usual. Right now his tone oozed good-humoured reason, and Lark waited for the crushingly outspoken punchline that she knew was coming.

'You're taking the step of disbelieving my colleague because of what? Your own belief that when men and women work together, men will inevitably take the lead? And that Lark is so brainwashed by that, that she doesn't even notice anything wrong?' Will smiled. 'I think you underestimate her...'

When Will returned to his office, after walking Pete to the door, Lark was pacing in front of the sofa. It wasn't making her feel any less angry.

'Stop pretending to be so nice to him, Will. Pete's just looking for conflict, when there isn't any. Does he have any actual qualifications in... anything?'

'I looked at his website and I didn't see any. Which doesn't mean that he's not very good at what he does, and I believe that he came highly recommended to Sir Terence.'

'You're giving him the benefit of the doubt when there isn't any.' Lark saw the hurt look in Will's eyes. 'I'm not angry with you...'

Somewhere, deep down, she was. She was angry with the handsome man who'd cooked her a fantastic dinner and who was stealing her heart. The one who'd kissed her goodbye, and made it last right through until the morning, when she'd woken from her dreams still feeling his touch. He should be unequivocally and unreasoningly on her side.

But his job was to do what he thought was right. Which involved putting the other side of the argument to her from time to time.

'I just wish you hadn't threatened to resign.' Lark couldn't help reproving him.

'What else was I going to do? We've already decided that patients are a no-go area when it comes to role-swapping, and if I can't do what's best for my patients then I shouldn't be here. Pete should never have brought that up again and I'm not going to minimise how important the principle is.'

He was right. Maybe Lark should have threatened to resign as well, but she hadn't wanted to be accused of following Will's lead.

'Why's he doing this, Will? This latest task...'

'Sir Terence has presumably told him that the trustees want to pick just one of us as a temporary CEO, so Pete has to find a way of overriding the way we work together, and making us compete. He couldn't make us question each other by intimating that I've been overruling you, and we won't budge on swapping roles where patients are involved. So he's asked us to work separately on proposals for further development for the charity.'

'And he really thinks we're going to do that. How's he ever going to know?'

Will shook his head. 'I think we'll do it because we said we would. I'm not going to agree to something and then break the rules, and I'm reckoning that you don't have that in mind either.'

'No, I don't. I wish I did—it would be so much easier.' Lark turned the corners of her mouth down.

'Not for me. Trusting you is non-negotiable, Lark.'

This was what it was all about. Two people trusting each other enough to be able to work seamlessly together, for the benefit of their patients. Two people who shouldn't be allowing this to come between them.

'You're right. I'm sorry, Will. I shouldn't be arguing with you because we both think the same way. We'll take the two proposals for further development that we have in hand, and split them up, one each. And we'll work on them alone, as we said we would. It may even get them done a bit faster...'

Will nodded, still looking a little downcast. Lark had forgotten something, and she knew exactly what that was. She walked towards him, laying her hand on the lapel of his jacket. 'And I'm going to break the rules now.'

'Yeah?'

She stood on her toes, kissing him. Suddenly Will's arm was around her waist, and he was kissing her with more passion than ever. Then he drew back.

It was over so quickly, but it meant everything. No stupid disagreement, blown out of all proportion by stress, was going to get in their way.

'Are we good?' Lark smiled up at him.

'I'd put it as *very* good. When we've finished with the afternoon clinic we can go home and beat effigies of Sir Terence and Pete with saucepans?'

Will could always make her laugh. Always propose a solution that worked emotionally, even if there might be a few loose ends on the practical side.

'What kind of effigies?'

'Whatever you like. We can stop off and buy melons, then draw faces on them. That'll make a very satisfying mess of my kitchen.'

'Or you could come back to mine, review my cooking utensils and what's in my fridge, and show me how to make a silk purse out of a sow's ear. Living well is the best revenge, isn't it? I'm assuming that steak and crepes aren't the only thing you can cook.'

Will grinned. 'That's very grown-up of you. Cooking will be no trouble at all, I have a repertoire.'

'I'm already looking forward to trying your repertoire out. Later…'

Lark's kitchen was the kind of challenge that could break a man. She had lots of fruit, wholemeal bread, brown rice, pasta, four different kinds of cheese and some sliced ham, which he reckoned she must use for sandwiches. Along with jars of apple sauce, burger sauce, salad dressing and a freezer full of made-up meals from the wholefoods freezer shop, that were nice but required nothing any more creative than switching the oven on. He found a can of stout beer in the back of a cupboard and an idea occurred to him.

'Okay, we'll start with the basics. Cheese on toast.'

'Like I've never had it before?'

She was getting the idea. Taking off his jacket and tie, Will rolled up his shirtsleeves. 'Mustard?' She must have mustard. Everyone had mustard.

'Of course! English or French?' Lark gave him an outraged look, and Will laughed.

By the time she returned from her bedroom, in a pair of casual trousers and a crimson sweater, the beer was already reducing in a pan. He gave her the easy job of grating the cheese and when she'd finished she crowded against him, curious to see what he was doing.

'You're in the way!'

'And *you're* meant to be showing me how to do this!' she flashed back at him.

Will gave in to the inevitable and handed over the wooden spoon, which clearly hadn't seen a lot of use. Leaving her to stir the cheese into the sauce he'd made, he cut the bread and put it into the toaster.

'Taste it.'

Lark dipped a spoon into the mixture and wrinkled her nose. 'It tastes like...cheese.'

'That's how it's supposed to taste. Now add a spoonful of mustard and a little of the beer... not too much...' He stopped her from tipping the lot into the mixture. 'Then taste it again.'

She was getting the idea. Lark tasted and then nodded. 'Bit more mustard.'

'Okay, add a little and then taste it again, until you have it right.'

'I'll be full by the time this is done.' Her elbow found his ribs and she nudged him gently.

'You're tasting, not eating.'

Lark wrinkled her nose and tipped half of the spoonful of the mixture back into the pan. Will knew he was hovering a little too close. But she didn't seem to mind, and the pleasure of watching her, feeling her, was too great to miss. A little more mustard, and some more beer, and she was satisfied.

'That's good. Want a taste?'

'I'll trust you. Keep stirring for a moment…' He fetched the toast, laying ham onto each slice, and then poured the viscous cheese mixture onto the top. 'A couple of minutes under the grill and it'll be done. Watch it while I get the plates…'

'Looks nice.' Lark had fetched the cutlery, leaving Will to pronounce the cheese properly toasted, and they sat down at the kitchen table together.

'What does it taste like, though?' Will watched while she sliced into the toast, and was rewarded by the look of sheer pleasure on her face as she took her first bite.

'That's perfect. Really scrummy.'

Scrummy was just what he'd been aiming for. They ate in silence, both clearing their plates.

'So...the trick is to keep tasting it, yes?' Lark asked.

'Yes. You start off with basic ingredients, and you need to know how much of those to add. But flavourings are a matter of adding a little until it's what you want.'

She nodded. 'You'll write a recipe for me? I'll be doing this again. Are we going to do something for afters?'

Dessert was another challenge, and Will was going to have to think about that for a moment. 'Okay. Have you got an empty notebook?'

She caught on immediately. Scrabbling around in a drawer to find the right scrap of paper when you'd decided to cook something took some of the creative pleasure out of the process for Will. A broad grin spread over her face.

'I've finally found your organised side, haven't I, Will. I definitely deserve something stupendous for afters now...'

He'd finally managed to come up with a spiced fruit dessert that met Lark's expectations of him, and then they'd washed the dishes together, returning Lark's kitchen to perfect order. *That* was part of the pleasure too. Then they'd moved through to the living area for coffee. Lark had finished painting the back wall and put the furniture back in place, and the colour scheme was really coming together.

They chatted over Lark's ideas for finishing off the job, and mulled over paint charts. She'd planned everything, and where the bolder colours threatened to take over, she'd thought of ways to break them up a little.

'It's going to look really great.'

'I hope so. It's something new for me, taking risks and adjusting things as I go.' Lark seemed uncharacteristically nervous about the results, when usually her forward planning didn't leave any room for surprises.

'Have I finally found your experimental side?' He received a tart look in reply and then Lark smiled.

'Maybe. This *is* a bit of a departure for me.'

It seemed so natural to put his arm around her shoulders. Comfort, maybe. Or approbation. Or just the sheer pleasure of having her close, feeling her move towards him to close the gap between them.

'But you're liking it?'

'Yes. As a matter of fact, I am.'

This was nice. Sharing things that they hadn't thought to share before. Carefully treading new ground that seemed full of the promise of delight. But however much Will wanted to take this further, he couldn't. Intimacy with a virtual stranger was so much more straightforward than intimacy with a friend.

'It's getting late. I should go.' He'd done what he'd come to do, and Lark had gone the whole evening without mentioning the challenges they faced at work. Will hadn't thought about them until now either. Maybe in the morning they'd both wake up and see it all in a different, less overwhelming perspective.

She didn't move. In fact, if anything, she seemed to shift a little closer. Will took a moment to appreciate that, and then took his arm from around her shoulders.

'Wait. Will...' He froze, unable to move away from her now. Too entranced with her to go back, and too much at a loss to go forward.

'We know far too much about each other not to talk about this.' Lark's practicality saved him from the agonies of indecision. 'I think we have to say it.'

He was lost now. Lark was braver than he was, and Will felt an exquisite relief wash over him. 'You have this all under control?'

She pulled a face. 'No. I... I know how I feel, though. I think—feel, actually—that I want to know you better. As if I can take a step in the dark with you, because I trust you. And I really want you to stay with me tonight.'

'I feel...a little afraid. Very awkward... I need to hear you say that you're ready to do this.' Will had meant to say that he wanted to be with her more than he'd wanted anything for a long time, but the truth slipped through before he could stop it.

Her eyes, golden in the sudden heat of the evening, gave him a taste of what it might be like to be with Lark all night.

'Probably not. But I want it so much that I don't care, and I trust that we can make things right between us. There's only one thing I have to know. Eloise...?' She pressed her lips together, as if she dared not even frame a question around the name. But this was something that Will *could* answer.

'It took me a long time to come to terms with the fact that I'd lost my future with Eloise. But I have, and I want to make a future with you now. One that's right for us.'

She hugged him wordlessly. Will coiled his arms around her shoulders, holding her tight. Lark seemed as breathless as he felt, caught up in the magnitude of what they'd just done.

'Would you like to see my bedroom? It's painted cream, so I think we're pretty safe in there.'

That was Lark's talent for taking the angst out of any given moment. He'd seen her do it with patients before, breaking what seemed impossible down into small, manageable steps. His familiarity with the technique made it all the sweeter. So much more like an act of love.

'Yes. Cream's good for a bedroom.'

'Sometimes...' She wriggled free of his embrace, giving him a mischievous smile that made Will's heart lurch. Then, taking him by the hand, she led him through to a closed door on the other side of the house.

Her bedroom was *very* cream. Soft, practical and... 'I think it could take a warmer colour.'

She looked round, as if she were seeing the room for the first time. Everything was neat and in order, with pale bedlinen and light oak furniture. 'Yes. You're right, it needs some warmth.'

That was something that Will could give now. He took her into his arms, kissing her, and felt her melt deliciously against him. Then she drew back, staring into his eyes as her fingers skimmed deftly across the all too thin cotton of his shirt. He let her do what she so clearly wanted, feeling the soft touch of her lips on his chest as she undid the buttons.

'Lark...' Her name felt so good, as if it belonged on his tongue. Will craved the sensation of kissing *her* skin.

Her hands moved, plucking at the hem of her top, suddenly awkward.

'Let me...' He whispered the words against her ear, feeling her relax again as she nodded. Will knew exactly what to do, and she gasped as he stripped off her top in one smooth action. Falling together into the unknown, he embraced her tightly, to let her know that he was there with her, all the way.

CHAPTER NINE

WILL WAS THE most exquisite lover. Kind and thoughtful, and yet never letting go of the passion that made everything he did so exciting. He'd undressed her as if it were the most natural thing in the world, and helped her when her fingers fumbled with his buttons.

He seemed to have no insecurities about his body, which was only natural since he looked so much better out of his clothes than in. Will kept himself in shape, often leaving work with his gym bag slung over his shoulder, and it was time well spent. And he lost no opportunity to make her feel beautiful, telling her exactly what he liked about her skin, her eyes…

There was exactly the right amount of time spent in foreplay, long enough to make her forget all of her doubts and fears. The donning of a condom from the drawer beside the bed was so seamless it was practically unnoticeable. He satisfied her completely, and then promptly found his own climax, while Lark was still enveloped in the rosy haze of hers.

And then he curled his arms around her, letting her use his chest as a pillow. Perfect. And…

'You okay?' She felt his lips brush her skin as he murmured the words.

'Yes!' Maybe she replied a little too defensively, because she felt him shift beside her, propping himself up on one elbow.

'But?'

How to break a man's confidence in one loving moment. They'd promised honesty, and she could be honest, without telling him the whole truth.

'It was wonderful, Will. Everything was perfect.'

'Go on.' Something in the clear blue of his eyes told her that he'd hoped for more too.

'I want *you*…' All of the uncertainties, and wrong moves. Everything that lay behind his charming exterior.

He nodded. 'What I really love about cooking is the tasting. Getting it wrong and then getting it right, inch by inch.'

'You won't let me into your kitchen, though. All I get to see is the perfect results.'

Will chuckled. 'Then I've made a mistake. How do you feel about getting this all wrong next time?' His body flexed against hers, as if it heartily approved of the idea.

'It's...a possibility. Is that what you want?'

He drew her closer, kissing the top of her head.

'I want unexpected possibilities, sweetheart.'

Those unexpected possibilities became realities far sooner than Lark had reckoned on. It was one thing for someone with the right knowledge to be able to estimate an average refractory period, and quite another to see Will's blue eyes blazing with desire as they touched and tasted their way to finding something new and different. She was sure that Will would have a bruise after having caught him with one of her flailing elbows, and when they could no longer stand those exquisite moments of play Lark managed to puncture the condom with her fingernail.

But the way his head snapped back and he gasped when she finally managed to roll the second one down over him, the note of desperation as she carefully checked it was in place... The way she lost herself suddenly, when Will moved a little too eagerly. It was real, and imperfect and far more than she'd ever imagined sex could be.

She came too soon, leaving him frustrated,

his eyes pleading for something that she guessed Will would never ask her for. Lark made him wait, carefully dropping kisses as she moved down his body. Making him come with her fingers and her mouth was a jagged, uncertain process of trial and error, but when she got it right he lost control, crying out her name.

This time he seemed exhausted, almost unable to move. Lark curled her body close to his and he laid his head on her shoulder.

'Did we do that right?' she murmured as she stroked his forehead.

'No. Let's do it like that again, shall we?' He caught her hand. 'Only next time without the elbows.'

Lark chuckled. 'Definitely. It's just that every part of me is so attracted to you. I dare say that was the problem with your chin and my nose.'

'Sorry about that. Is kissing all right?'

Lark snuggled a little closer. 'Kissing's great. Only don't kiss me as if you're about to make love to me again, because I know you can't.'

He brushed his lips against her cheek. 'That was the best...the *very* best sex...'

'I loved it, Will. Every single moment. Can we sleep now?'

He curled his body around her. There were no barriers left between them now, only new places to explore. 'I was hoping you might say that...'

* * *

They both slept soundly. Will woke with her in his arms, happy to watch the hands on the clock crawl from ten o'clock to half past, and then Lark began to stir.

He'd had the best of motives, but had started out doing everything wrong. If Will hadn't known Lark so well, he might have accepted her reassurances that everything was fine and continued to hide behind experience and timing to ensure that everything between them went exactly to plan.

But Lark had overturned all that. She'd torn down his barriers, refusing to accept anything other than the man who hid behind them. Real passion could be awkward, badly timed and frustrating. But it was *real* and that made it the best thing in the world.

Will had learned one important lesson. Getting things right with Lark would take a while, probably longer than the foreseeable future. And he was ready for that now. Ready to spend the time it took to become an honest lover instead of just a good one.

'Will you spend the day with me?' Lark had opened her eyes now, and he couldn't wait to ask the question.

'Good morning to you too,' she chided him

gently. 'And I'd love to spend the day with you. What shall we do?'

Will thought for a moment. 'I've got to go home for a change of clothes. Come with me, and we'll play things by ear...'

There was no particular reason to go anywhere else after they'd returned to his flat, so Will showed Lark how easy it was to make maple and pecan bread with a bread maker and she'd sealed her relationship with his kitchen by examining the contents of his cupboards and drawers. They lounged on the sofa together, while the bread maker hummed quietly in the kitchen, and after fresh buttered bread and hot chocolate they'd gravitated towards the bedroom. Talking, negotiating everything about this new phase in their lives.

And then, at four in the afternoon, they found their rhythm. Lark had undressed slowly for him, and he'd undressed for her. Will had propped himself up against the pillows, and Lark was astride him on his lap. Naked, and joined in the most intimate way. Will stretched one arm around her hips, stopping her from forcing the pace by moving too suddenly, and she squeezed the muscles that cradled him.

'I can't take too much more of that, sweetheart.' Lark had probably already guessed that from the sharp gasp that had escaped his lips.

'Good to know. I want this to last.'

So did Will. He reached for the dish by the side of the bed, that contained halved strawberries. Held one against her lips, then watched her savour it while he licked the taste of strawberries from his fingers.

She gasped as he cupped her breast. 'I'm not sure how much of *that* I can take, Will. Not so fast...'

This was all about voicing every part of their desire. Harnessing it until it could no longer be contained. They were slowly working towards something that was beyond any of the limits that either of them had breached before. That should be terrifying, but right now it was all-consuming.

'How's this?' He moved beneath her, sitting up a little straighter so that he could hold her hips more tightly against his and stop Lark from hastening their pleasure. 'Would my making you beg be of any interest to you?'

Her eyes darkened, the gold gleaming a little more brilliantly in contrast. 'Yes, it would. Does it interest you at all?'

'I was hoping you might ask.' Will brushed his lips against hers. They tasted strawberry sweet. 'Although you've turned me into a complete walkover, so I'll be begging soon, whether you like it or not.'

Lark leaned forward, whispering in his ear. 'Hold out, Will. You want to hold out, don't you?'

His hand found her breast again, and he felt her body. 'I want to. First, you show me how long *you* can hold out...'

Will had made love to her for what seemed like days. Hours, at least. And somewhere, some time between the first awakening of passion and the final quiet after the storm, they'd found each other.

It had been lifechanging. They were moving past the way things had been and into new territory. That had always been too terrifying for Lark to even consider, but a whole weekend where good food, good love and an amazing friendship seemed blended together in one blissful passage of time made taking the risks worth it.

On Monday morning they stood in the queue at the coffee shop together. Not touching, but maybe their body language betrayed that they were lovers. Caught up with Will in a bubble.

'Maybe I'll drink my coffee here.' Lark looked around the busy coffee shop. There were plenty of empty tables—at this time in the morning most people wanted takeaway.

'You're *trying* to be late for work? That's a first.'

She shrugged. 'You know. Arriving together.'

'We arrive together all the time, particularly on a Monday morning.' Will frowned. 'In fact, I think *not* arriving together might be more suspicious. Or more particularly contriving not to arrive together. If someone we know happens to pop in here and sees one of us drinking coffee instead of going straight up to the office, then that's a pretty conclusive indication that something's going on.'

'You've thought about this, haven't you.' Lark bit her tongue, but not before Will shot her a rueful look. His recent history with women was—history. They'd talked about it and Will had told her that this was different. But she couldn't help feeling a little insecure at times.

'I guess so.' He turned his blue-eyed gaze on her, and suddenly Lark had no doubt at all about Will's commitment to her. 'Would it be too old-fashioned to say that I want to protect you?'

Lark grinned at him. 'I hope that protecting your friends never goes out of fashion.'

'Good point. Did you have anything in mind with regard to protecting me, then?'

He had a way of turning everything on its

head and making it feel shining and new. 'Don't you worry, Will. You're quite safe with me.'

No one batted an eye when they walked into the office together, although going to their separate offices and staying there might have raised a few eyebrows. They'd decided that the challenge that Pete had set them—to each work alone on one of the projects that the charity was considering taking forward—would be handled strictly in terms of their agreement. Will would take the proposal for workshops for first responders, aimed at helping them to avoid the very real risks associated with sleep disruption and recurrent migraine, and Lark was going to consider a community outreach scheme for schools, to understand childhood migraine better. Working alone might be a good exercise for both of them.

And so it went. Pete had called, wondering if it might be best to postpone his next session for a week, so that they could concentrate on their proposals, and Will had accepted the idea immediately. Lark had wondered whether Pete sensed that the sessions weren't going too well, but she didn't care because that was one Friday that they didn't have to contend with spending an hour away from the things they really needed to do. There was plenty to keep them busy, follow-ups from helpline calls, liaison with home visitors and, of course, their afternoon clinics. But their evenings and weekends were spent together, even if they were partly taken up with the proposals that they were both writing.

'So...you're nearly finished?' Will looked up from his laptop. Lark was propped up on pillows, her own laptop in front of her, and he'd retreated to the foot of the large bed, facing her. When Will made a promise, he kept it.

'Thirty-four pages.'

He grinned. 'Forty-five.'

Lark frowned at him. 'Forty-five?' Maybe she should change the formatting of her document, so that it at least hit the forty-page mark.

'One and a half spacing. Easier to read. And I've mentioned a few possibilities in the introduction that aren't practical just yet, but might be in the future. I might take them out.'

'There's nothing *wrong* with blue-sky thinking, Will. No one's asking you to stop doing the things you're really good at.'

'You think I'm trying too hard to be you?' He shook his head suddenly. 'On second thoughts, don't answer that. It could be construed as collusion.'

Lark hit *save* and snapped the lid of her laptop shut. 'We work together, Will. Doing one task separately doesn't mean that we can't talk about general principles.'

He nodded thoughtfully. 'Okay. So what do you reckon?'

'I think it's Saturday evening and you could stop working now. Take your clothes off and bring your blue-sky thinking over here...'

Will feigned outrage. 'You reckon that seduction's going to give you an advantage, do you?'

There *was* an element of competition about this. Working together demanded a lot of give and take, and it was usually impossible for either of them to claim full ownership of the planning documents they produced. But working separately invited comparisons, and they'd been joking about those all week.

'I'll give it a go. It might work to my advantage.'

Will closed his laptop and leaned to pick hers up, stowing them both away on the table next to the bed. 'So what are the chances that I'll read what you've done while you're sleeping?'

None, probably. Will could be frighteningly honest at times.

'You think you'll be awake to do that?'

He kissed her. Tenderness spiced with the heat of competition was even more exciting than Lark had expected.

'Let's find out, shall we?'

CHAPTER TEN

SOMEHOW, AFTER A late night working on their proposals, and an even later night spent trying to wear each other out, Will had woken early. He'd taken it for granted that he'd grown out of that sudden burst of energy that accompanied a new relationship, but Lark had shown him differently. Maybe the energy came from the realisation that this time he was prepared to fall in love. Not just fall, Will felt that at any moment he was going to take a running jump.

They emailed both their proposals to Sir Terence three days later, making sure to co-ordinate carefully so that both emails didn't turn up in his inbox at the same time. On Friday evening, when they met with Pete, both Will and Lark expected that should be enough.

'I heard from Sir Terence.' Pete had barely sat down at the small conference table in Lark's office before he dropped his latest bombshell. Will saw Lark straighten a little in her seat.

'He hasn't come back to us yet.' Will decided that a reminder that Pete wasn't actually a part of the decision-making process might be in order.

'He hasn't distributed the material to the other trustees yet.' Pete brushed his comment to one side. 'This is unofficial feedback.'

'Generally speaking, *any* feedback, official or otherwise, is treated as confidential until it's been discussed between Howard and the board.' Lark voiced his own thoughts.

'Sir Terence has spoken to me because this directly pertains to the work we're doing together.' Pete dismissed Lark's comment and Will felt a prickle of outrage run up his spine. 'Your two proposals were both of high quality and strikingly similar.'

'You've read them?' Will tried not to make the comment sound like a challenge, but clearly it did because Pete's usually calm demeanour broke for a moment.

'No, as Lark pointed out, the documents are part of the charity's confidential decision-making process. I've just given you the full extent of the feedback I received from Sir Terence. This is a full disclosure environment, and anything that's said here is confidential as well.'

In that case...

'If you want full disclosure, then I think it's

fair to say that neither Lark or I are particularly happy with the increasing amount of time we're spending on the tasks you're setting.' Will glanced at Lark and she nodded in agreement. 'We're only here two days a week, and we're trying to run a charity, care for patients who come to us for help, and cover for our CEO. We can do it, but it's not helpful to give us unnecessary work at the moment. And, as we've pointed out before, our patients and the communities we serve must come first.'

'Of course. Noted.' Will saw Lark roll her eyes. This seemed to be Pete's answer to almost anything that challenged him. 'But I think you'll find this next suggestion fun…'

'Fun? Fun!' Lark had been bottling this up all the way back to Will's place. But now he was sprawled on the sofa, watching as she paced back and forth in front of the hearth.

'It's insupportable, Will. What are we a pair of…?'

'Performing seals?'

'Yes, exactly. We're being treated as if we're a pair of performing seals. And what does this Leadership Day involve, anyway?'

'Pete said that we'd be handling unexpected situations. I suppose if they tell you what they are, then it's not unexpected, is it.' Will turned the corners of his mouth down.

'I suppose not. It's too bad—we have things to do on Sunday.' Cook. Eat. Make love. They were things to do, weren't they?

'Do you believe that thing about a cancelled booking?'

'Not for a minute. This is something that Sir Terence has dreamed up with Pete. No doubt we'll be marked on everything we do, and that's going to be part of the decision about who becomes temporary CEO.'

He nodded. 'Yeah, I don't think any of this just happened. Perhaps Sir Terence thinks that having just one of us to deal with will mean he gets his own way a little more often than he does with Howard. And that whoever gets picked will feel they owe him something.'

'I hadn't thought of that. You're right, of course, and that makes it even more annoying.' Lark stopped pacing because it wasn't making her feel any better. Being in Will's arms always made her feel better and she perched on the side of the sofa, next to him. 'Tell me he's not going to get away with this.'

He pulled her down and kissed her. 'He's not going to get away with it. He can't make us compete with each other if we don't want to, and I'm not even sure I want to be a temporary CEO. I'd rather enjoy working under you.'

'Oh, and leave me to deal with Sir Terence. That's not nice.'

'Howard obviously kept him under control. I have every confidence in your ability to be firm.' He kissed her again.

'Stop kissing me, Will!'

'You've heard of angry sex, haven't you?'

'Yes, and angry sex is when we're angry with each other. Not when I'm angry and you're trying to convince everyone, including yourself, that everything's okay.'

He gave her a wry smile. 'Busted. It's not okay, is it. I feel just as wretched about it as you do.'

'Thank you.' His admission took the edge off Lark's anger. 'I know that's hard for you to say.'

'It's time. I don't want to keep living the way I have done, keeping everyone at arm's length. Especially you, Lark.'

She hugged him, feeling his heart beat against hers. 'Let's look at it logically, shall we? It's too late to contact Sir Terence or any of the other trustees this evening, and they won't thank us for stirring things up over the weekend. We'll play along, go on Sunday, and then decide what to do on Monday. Then make a joint approach to the whole Board of Trustees.'

'Are you being deliberately conciliatory? That was what I was going to suggest.' He wound his arms around her shoulders, enveloping her in his warmth.

'I think it's the right thing to do.' Lark kissed him. 'And yes, I'm being deliberately conciliatory. We can save the heavy artillery for when we know exactly what's happening, eh?'

'Good plan. And in the meantime I'll do my best to make it up to you for losing our lazy Sunday together.'

'It's not your fault, Will. You don't have to make anything up to me.'

He chuckled, whispering in her ear, and Lark's eyes widened. 'You can make baked Alaska?'

'Usually. Sometimes it goes wrong and ends up something like a hot Eton Mess.'

'I like Eton Mess as well. And I love a little trial and error with you…'

He dropped a kiss onto her lips. 'You want to make a start, then…?'

At eight o'clock on Sunday morning, after an hour's drive out of London, they drew into a wide, curved access road. The hotel was housed in an older building, which had once been a grand country mansion, and the conference centre in a modern annexe. Will followed the signs, heading for the car park.

'Nice place.' He got out of the car, looking around him. Despite having already made their lunch choices, in response to the emails they'd both received yesterday, they still didn't know what the day ahead held.

In the shining, smartly decorated interior of the conference centre their names were taken and they were asked to check in their phones, before being directed to a large room, with comfortable seats arranged in a circle at the far end, alongside a table that was laid out with drinks and pastries. Two men were already there, talking intently, and a smart middle-aged woman was quietly drinking coffee while she surveyed the room.

Lark gravitated to the coffee, pouring two cups, and Will caught the woman's eye. He smiled and she smiled back.

'Hi, I'm Will.'

'Anna. Do you know what we'll be doing today? All I got was an instruction to be here at eight-thirty, and to dress for physical activity.'

Good to know. At least he and Lark weren't the only people in the dark.

'No idea. I'm here with my colleague, Lark Foster. We work for a medical charity.'

'Really? How fascinating.' Anna smiled at

him. 'I'm an accountant. What area of medicine does your charity deal with?'

Will couldn't help a grin. No doubt Lark would tell him that this was a version of how he usually introduced himself, moving quickly past the details about himself and showing interest in the person he was talking with.

'We provide information and support for people who are affected by migraine.'

'Then you must meet a lot of people who are personally interested in your work. I've been suffering with migraines for years...' Anna turned the corners of her mouth down. Will reached into the back pocket of his jeans and proffered his card.

'I dare say you have it pretty much under control by now, then?'

Anna shrugged, 'Ninety-five percent of the time. Whenever we go on holiday my husband plans in a bit of sightseeing on his own for the first couple of days, while I'm lying in a darkened room wishing I was at home.'

'That's not uncommon—you've been working hard and you feel fine, then you get some time off and start to relax and it hits you? I used to get a version of that, when I went through a period of not sleeping during the week and then sleeping more heavily at weekends.'

Anna nodded. 'I always think that's one of

the more mean-spirited sides of it. You get some time off and then it hits you.' She tucked the card into the pocket of her immaculate jeans. 'I'll take a look at your website, Will.'

Always use a person's name, at least once. That way, you can remember it, and the conversation becomes more personal. Lark would be suppressing a smile by now, ready to whisper to him later that he'd met his match in Anna.

'Thank you. There's a section on "Holiday Migraine" and we're always interested in hearing from people. It's something we'd like to learn more about…' Will jumped as he felt Lark nudge him. She was balancing two cups and a selection of mini pastries on a plate, and Will took the coffee from her before she spilled it.

'Hi, I'm Lark.' She held out the plate.

'Thanks, these do look nice. I'm Anna.' Anna smiled, choosing a pastry. 'What a pretty name.'

Lark chuckled. 'I'm not sure that my parents thought too much about the expectations it carries. Some people take it for granted that six o'clock in the morning is my best time.'

Anna laughed and the two women started to chat, Anna gesturing towards Lark's serviceable cargo pants, saying that she wished she'd had something in her wardrobe with roomy pockets, since today was about being ready for any eventuality. By the time they got to exchanging information about what they did for a living, Lark's irrepressible warmth was already in evidence between them.

A man had just entered the room, closely followed by a woman, both of them looking around, trying to read the room. It was time for him to circulate and see whether he could find out a bit more about what today might hold...

'Hit me with it, then.' Twenty minutes later he found Lark at his side, and Will automatically stepped back from the five other members of the group.

'Adrian's the headmaster of a private secondary school. Listens to everyone and thinks about what they say, but he doesn't betray too much of what he's thinking. Molly's a lawyer, and she's ambitious, very focused on getting ahead. Graham's in manufacturing, but he's keeping everything else very close to his chest. My guess is that his word is law in his workplace and he's not used to being questioned on any of his decisions.'

Lark nodded. 'And Evan?'

'He's built up his own marketing company and is busy stressing how important he is. I reckon that Anna's the most high-powered...'

'You're good... And you make it seem so effortless.' She'd said that before, but then it had been *very good*. A thrill tingled through Will's veins as she smiled up at him.

'Just *good*?'

'You can't be *very* good at everything, Will.' She shot him a look of reproof and Will decided that on balance it was better to be very good at the things that pleased Lark. Even if the thought threatened to bring him to his knees.

'Anna's a director at...one of the big accounting firms...' Lark frowned, clearly trying to remember which one, and when Will supplied the name of the most influential she nodded. 'And you're a consultant neurologist.'

He could almost see what she was thinking. Lark's habit of assuming that everyone else was more important than she was, wasn't going to help her today.

'And your job is to save lives. If I was going to choose who I wanted to lead me...'

'Okay. Point taken.' Lark frowned. 'Don't you think that sizing everyone up is all a bit...calculating?'

'Of course it is. This is a leadership course, and the first thing you need to do when leading others, or being led by them, is to size them up. Why do you think we've been put into a room alone together for the last half hour?'

'Oh. I was thinking they were just giving us a chance to settle in and eat all the pastries.'

Lark's head turned as a young man and woman entered the room, wearing matching sweatshirts with the conference centre logo on the back, and started to beckon to everyone to join them in the circular seating area.

She puffed out a breath. 'I think it's time to get to work now, though...'

Lark was looking a little nervous and Will sat down next to her, trying to radiate some confidence in her direction. Amy and Ben introduced themselves as their course co-ordinators for the day, and told them that they would each be leading the others in completing one task. Each task was expected to take about an hour and there were no rules, apart from keeping everyone safe. Then they were pitched straight in to the first task, which Evan would lead.

Evan rose with an air of showing his fellow course attendees how it was done, and they followed Ben into an adjoining room. There was a small lobby and in front of them a single access revolving door, the glass panels covered with black baize, which concealed whatever was beyond. Ben wordlessly gave Evan a set of key cards and a clipboard.

No instructions. Everyone was looking around at everyone else, obviously wondering what they'd be facing on the other side of the door.

'Okay...' Evan had read through the instruction sheet fixed to the clipboard, and now seemed ready to start. 'We have to go one at a time, and when each person makes their way through the exit door, a buzzer sounds in here and the next person can go inside. Who'd like to try that out and report back?'

Leading from the back was one way of doing it. Evan's gaze moved from one face to the next, clearly waiting for the first person to cave in and volunteer.

'I'll go.' Will stepped forward at the same moment that Lark did, and he nudged her out of the way. She knew as well as he did that Evan's tactic could send the most vulnerable member of the group in first, and that generally speaking it was better to play to people's strengths than their weaknesses. And Will didn't care if he seemed overprotective. Lark wasn't going through that door until he'd seen what was on the other side of it.

'Great, thanks.' Evan gave him the key card and scribbled his name down on the pad. 'I'll time you...'

'Whatever it is, don't rush it.' He heard Lark murmur the words and nodded in acknowledgement, then inserted the key card into the lock, pushing the revolving doors. Suddenly he was plunged into complete darkness.

Okay. That was unexpected. Holding out his hands, he explored the space to his right and felt his fingers brush against something, which on further investigation turned out to be a solid, padded wall. There was another to his left and Will moved forward carefully, one hand in front of his face and the other touching the wall.

As his eyes adjusted to the darkness, he saw a muted light up ahead, and he counted his steps as he moved towards it. Turning a corner, he found himself surrounded by mirrors that reflected multiple shadowy images of himself back at him. Looking around, he could just see a camera trained on him, and he nodded upwards it. Clearly the organisers had taken some trouble to make sure that people going through here were monitored.

Further along, and in darkness again, something brushed against his shoulder and he jumped, raising his hand to find soft door streamers in his way. Then there was a locked door, which he had to find the key for in the darkness. He let it close behind him, then opened it again, checking whether he was able to go back, and storing the information away in case he needed it later. After that, a maze of turns and dead ends, where he completely lost his bearings. More by luck than anything else, he found his way through to another door, which opened when he used the key card in his pocket. Will stepped outside, blinking in the sunlight.

'You made it. Everything okay?' Amy was waiting for him on a wide veranda that stretched the length of the back of the building.

Everything was just fine. Apart from the fact that his three main priorities at the moment were keeping the charity running, seeing patients and spending time alone with Lark, and he wasn't doing any of these things. But that wasn't Amy's fault.

'Yeah, it's all good. You have cameras in there?'

Amy grinned. 'Yep, thermal imaging so that I can watch everyone through.' She turned the screen of the tablet she was holding towards him, and Will saw the blue outline of a figure in the first of a series of small windows, the red heat of its hands reaching out as his had done.

'He's let someone else in, before I had a chance to report back?' Will couldn't keep the tone of disbelief out of his voice.

Amy shrugged, turning the corners of her mouth down in silent agreement. 'Everyone does this differently. You should be back before the next person goes through...' Her head was bent now, watching the image on her tablet, and Will hurried away.

There was no need to worry. The darkness

had been challenging but there were safeguards in place. But something about the jerky movements of the small image on the screen had suggested panic rather than disorientation, and that bothered Will.

What bothered him more was that he'd be willing to bet that Lark had volunteered to go next. She was used to going into potentially hazardous situations so that other people didn't have to, and he'd already had to stop her from going first into the unknown.

Six heads turned towards him as he burst back into the lobby, after having walked the length of the building to get back in through the main entrance.

Evan beamed at him. 'Three minutes and forty seconds. Your friend will have to get a move on to beat that.'

It wasn't all about the competition. Will ignored Evan, making for Ben. 'Where is she?'

Ben's eyes flipped to the screen of his tablet. 'Looks as if she's standing still.'

'Let me see...'

Ben handed him the tablet, clearly a little concerned, and Will saw that Lark was standing in the hall of mirrors. In the low light, she looked as if she were talking to herself.

'I'll go and fetch her.'

Ben nodded, taking a flashlight from his belt and handing it to Will.

'No you don't, we might lose marks for that.' Evan was bristling with indignation. '*I'm* the team leader and that's my decision to make.'

Will ignored him, making for the revolving door. As he swiped his key card he heard Anna speak, cool steel in her tone.

'Be quiet, Evan. Will's more qualified to make this decision than you are...'

In the beam of light, Will could see the corridor in front of him, covered in dark padded material. 'Lark...' he called to her softly.

She didn't answer. Then he heard her whimper quietly.

'Stay right where you are, Lark. Let me find you.' The slight glow up ahead told him that he'd soon be amongst the subtle lighting around the mirrors.

As he turned the corner he saw her. Standing still, her hands up to her face. Something was wrong, and Will shone the flashlight at her feet so that she could see where she was and what surrounded her.

'I'm okay.' As soon as he reached her she flung her arms around him, holding on tight to his sweater. Clearly she didn't realise they were being watched, and at this moment Will didn't care. 'I don't like the dark all that much.'

Yet another thing he'd just learned about her. He'd assumed that her insistence on leaving the hall light on outside the bedroom was because they were still unused to the layout of each other's homes.

'I think there's a mutiny going on outside. Should we go back and save Evan?'

She laughed suddenly. 'As long as they're not going to make him walk the plank in the next five minutes, it's probably best if we turn the light out and I finish the course, eh? Then at least he can say he got everyone through.'

'You're sure? Don't do anything you're uncomfortable with, just for him.'

'I'll be okay if I know you're with me.'

That he couldn't resist. Will still wasn't entirely sure whether a person could overcome their fears for love, but he'd been willing to give it a try, and now it appeared Lark was too.

'Okay. You're ready…?'

'Not quite.' Will felt her body move against his. 'A kiss first?'

'Uh… That's all I can think about right now, but there are cameras in here.'

Lark let go of him, stepping back. 'Oh! Thermal imaging, you mean?'

Will nodded, trying not to grin as he handed her the flashlight. Lark switched it off, looking around in the half-light to find the camera and waving at it, giving a thumbs-up to show that everything was okay. She clipped the flashlight to her belt, and then smiled up at him.

'Stop it, Will. File those notions away for later.'

'You can tell what I'm thinking?' Will couldn't quite shake the idea of being surrounded by mirrors, watching multiple images of themselves making love. Or of being able to see the heat that radiated from them as they kissed.

'When it's about sex, yes.'

Good to know. And it was good to see that Lark was getting over the fright she'd had over being plunged into the darkness without any warning. She took his hand, walking to the edge of the pool of light around the mirrors.

'Don't give me any clues…'

'Why not? If Evan had waited until I got back, you would have heard the exact layout, along with everyone else.'

'If you can puzzle your way through this, then so can I. Give a woman a chance to compete with you, eh?' Lark squeezed his hand, stepping into the darkness.

CHAPTER ELEVEN

THE DARKNESS WASN'T as terrifying as it had been the first time. Feeling Will's hand in hers gave Lark the confidence to find the key to the locked door, instead of sinking to the ground in despair, and the maze was a piece of cake because it was a simple labyrinth based on the age-old principle of turning always to the right. They walked out into the sunshine, then hurried back to the rest of the team, to find that comparative peace had broken out.

Will gave a description of the first part of the course, and when he seemed a little vague about the succession of turns required to get through the maze, Lark was able to close her eyes and visualise them more exactly. That helped everyone through quickly and without incident, and Lark saw Anna roll her eyes when Evan shook Will's hand, congratulating him on his contribution to a great team effort.

Then they all started to have fun. Adrian's

task was to assemble a steam-driven vehicle with the help of only a diagram, and somehow he managed to draw everyone together, dividing up the seemingly impossible task into manageable chunks. The engine was ready surprisingly quickly, and when it was taken outside for a test run, everyone cheered when the wheels started to turn and it edged forward.

'Do you think I should apologise to everyone? For messing up the first challenge.' Lark had retreated to a corner when they broke for coffee, and Will had followed her, his protective bulk suddenly seeming very welcome.

He frowned. 'No, I don't think you have anything to apologise for. We're all afraid of something, and you conquered your particular fear and finished the course. That's walking the extra mile for the team in my book.'

'I just...' Lark shrugged. 'I think if I'd expected to be plunged into complete darkness I might have handled it better though. It came as a surprise, and I don't much like the unexpected.'

Will puffed out a breath. 'You're not going to let this go, are you.'

'Not sure I can.' Lark didn't know why.

'Well... I know you like to plan things out, and you're very good at it. But isn't an aversion to the unexpected something of a disadvantage when you're a first responder?'

Lark shook her head. 'That's not the same at all. We're trained for the situations we encounter, and we can make a difference.'

'May I ask...?' Will was looking at her thoughtfully.

'Anything. You know that, don't you?'

His gaze suddenly captured hers. Lark wondered whether it would actually be possible to live in that gaze, needing nothing else.

'Were you there when Robyn was injured?'

The question took her breath away. Lark remembered that day so clearly, the shock as she'd seen her sister fall from one of the swings at the local playground, lying still on the ground. The awful fear, as she'd realised that there was nothing she could do to make Robyn better, and the way the darkness had lifted when she'd seen the ambulance draw up beside the playground, and two green-clad superheroes hurrying towards them.

'You think...that's why I became a paramedic?' It didn't seem that much of a leap now that Lark thought about it.

He smiled, shaking his head. She'd come to appreciate Will's smile even more now, since it was no longer something that he used to convince everyone around him that everything was perfectly fine, but something that had to be earned.

'Howard once told me that when you were at university, you were the best student he'd ever seen. We're all inspired to do what we do by something, but the commitment required is a life choice.'

'Thank you.' Lark couldn't give Will any answers right now, she had to think about what he'd said, but she knew he'd wait. 'This course... perhaps it's more worthwhile than we thought it was going to be.'

He thought for a moment. 'Yes, I think it is. Although probably not quite in the way that Sir Terence supposed. We're not trying to outdo each other, are we?'

'Aren't we? Who insisted on going first through the revolving door?'

'And who insisted on turning off the flashlight and finishing the course, despite being terrified of the dark?'

Fair enough. Lark's first thought had been that if Will could do it so could she, and competing with him did add a layer of excitement to any task.

'You're right. I think I *am* doing better than you.' Lark knew that Will couldn't resist the challenge.

'Yeah? You'll have to have more up your sleeve than that to beat me.'

'Watch and learn, Will...'

***

Molly had micro-managed her way through the first ten minutes of her challenge before Anna tactfully took her to one side for a conversation, and her tension relaxed suddenly. Then it was Will's turn and with the aid of a whiteboard, pens and an irresistible smile, he managed to spur the team on in finding all of the required items of a scavenger hunt.

None of this was supposed to be a competition, but the grin he'd given her when they sat down for lunch, in the pleasant surroundings of the conference centre's restaurant, belied that.

'You've set the bar high.' Lark smiled at him. At first sight, a scavenger hunt didn't have a great deal of application to what Will did in either of his jobs. But actually, enthusing the people around him, encouraging them and playing to their strengths, however trivial a task seemed, was something he did well. He'd make a great CEO for Migraine Community Action.

'Is that an admission of defeat?' His smile told her that he thought it was nothing of the sort.

'Never. I'd rather slay a dragon than a mouse.'

'Nice to know. I'd rather *be* a dragon than a mouse.' He was still chuckling as he turned to chat to Evan, who seemed to have got over his grumpiness at being sidelined in his own challenge, and had made a success of his part in Will's challenge. Will had a way of turning things around and finding common ground in a conflict.

Talk over lunch turned from work to personal, as the team began to bond. Anna observed that the later tasks would be easier than the earlier ones, in a pointed reference which Lark took as a peace offering for Evan, and made sure she voiced her agreement.

Ben smiled. 'Yeah. We know that everyone bonds much better for the later tasks. We take that into account.'

'So they *are* marking us on what we do here...' Will murmured quietly to her.

Before Lark could answer, she heard a shriek from the veranda outside the restaurant. Amy had been sitting drinking coffee with someone, who was now sprawled on the ground.

'Lark! Help...'

One glance told her that the 'man' was actually a full body CPR dummy, dressed up in jeans and a hoodie. But, all the same, the sudden switch from relaxation to purposeful single-mindedness was real.

'This one's mine. Round everyone up, Will...' Lark got to her feet, running through the open doors which led onto the veranda, where Amy was now bending over the dummy.

The dummy wasn't realistic enough to display any symptoms and Lark relied on Amy, who was making a realistic show of panic, to find out what had happened. By the time the others arrived, and Will joined her next to the dummy, she'd unzipped its jacket, gone through the motions of clearing airways and had started CPR.

'I've done this a hundred times...' It didn't seem particularly difficult to just do it again while everyone stood around and watched.

'Make it your own, then.' Will could always be relied on to challenge her and an idea occurred to Lark.

'Take over with the CPR, will you...'

Lark got to her feet, while Will concentrated on the task she'd given him. The dummy was a high-end model which showed a response when CPR was given correctly, and all he had to do was keep the LED in its forehead alight, but the effort involved in that was real.

'This is just an exercise, isn't it? No one's hurt, and no one's going to die.' He heard Lark's voice. 'As a paramedic, I'm going to tell you that it's not. Because this is my chance to show you all what to do when someone suffers a cardiac arrest for real. The whole purpose of the next hour is that this team saves a life. Maybe not today, but one day.'

Nice one. Will allowed himself a smile at Lark's audacity and glanced at Ben, whose face was impassive. He and Amy didn't give much away during the challenges.

'Has anyone had CPR training before?'

'I have.' Will heard Adrian's voice.

'That's great. Go and help Will, please. Will, make sure that Adrian's doing everything correctly. Keeping CPR up can be exhausting, even if you're a fit man like Will, and if you can find someone to help all the better. But never leave someone who's in cardiac arrest alone…'

'I don't think I'm strong enough…' He heard an unfamiliar note of uncertainty in Anna's voice.

'That's okay, Anna. You do your best. If someone's heart has stopped, then they're dying. Anything you can do to reverse that is better than nothing, and I'll show you how to use your own weight to maximise your compressions. Now—does anyone know if there's an automatic defibrillator here?'

Will sat back on his heels, watching as Adrian took over the chest compressions on the dummy. Lark would have noticed the cabinet on the wall behind the receptionist's desk, it was second nature to her.

'In reception.' Evan spoke up, and Lark nodded.

'Well spotted. Would you fetch it please,

Evan. It's good to make a habit of looking out for the green and white sign when you're in an unfamiliar place, just as you might notice fire extinguishers...'

Lark took the team through all the steps, explaining exactly what Will was doing. Everyone was engaged and asking questions and if Will had thought he could compete with this... She was walking all over him. His enjoyment at the thought might be letting Sir Terence down badly, but Will didn't care.

Then Lark gave everyone the chance to practise CPR on the dummy and use the automatic defibrillator themselves. When it was Graham's turn he hesitated, scrunching his fingers up to avoid touching the manikin's chest. Lark grinned at him.

'I can see why you're doing that, Graham, but you're not going to be able to do the compressions properly.' She sat back on her heels, making sure she had everyone's attention. 'Will, would you demonstrate the position of your right hand on your own chest, please.'

He could see where this was going. And it was a very valid point. People who weren't medically trained were sometimes confronted by the idea of touching a stranger in what would usually be considered an inappropriate way. He placed the heel of his hand two inches above his sternum and spread his fingers out.

'You'll see where Will's hand is. Now, if I do the same thing...' Lark's fingers spread across her left breast and Will tried not to grin. The whole purpose of the exercise was to convince everyone *not* to be embarrassed. 'Remember that you're trying to save my life, so I'm not going to mind. And Molly, can you help us with any legal pointers?'

Molly smiled. 'Yes, the law does protect you in this kind of situation...'

It had been a good day. As they walked together across the car park, Lark was still buzzing from the goodbyes.

'I thought for a moment that you were going to ask *me* to demonstrate where I'm supposed to touch you during CPR...' Will grinned down at her.

'It crossed my mind. I might have done if your hand hadn't been right there last night.' Now that they were lovers, Will's smile would have blown any attempt at professional distance to pieces.

He chuckled. 'Because I only became aware of the fact that you're the most gorgeous woman I know two weeks ago?'

'Stop with the charm, Will...'

He spread his hands in a gesture of rebuff. 'It's a matter of fact. I always thought you were gorgeous. Just unattainable for someone like me.'

His unspoken question hung in the air between them. There was no point in denying it...

'I thought you were gorgeous too. But since you were my friend, I had far too much to lose.'

And now? She'd been Will's friend and colleague for years, but *lovers* was already becoming more important. Lark had been telling herself that the three weren't mutually exclusive, but it was so easy to become lost in her desire for him, and that felt a little scary. She decided it would be best to change the subject.

'Anna's challenge was fun.' The conference centre had its own climbing wall, and Anna had been tasked with getting each member of the team to the top of it.

'You looked as if you could have done with some inappropriate touching when you got stuck on that tricky bit, right at the top.' Will smiled down at her. 'Although you still made it before I did.'

'By two seconds.'

'Three. And I'm man enough to acknowledge when I'm beaten.'

'I notice you stopped to help Molly,' Lark teased him.

He shrugged. 'There's nothing inappropriate about grabbing Molly's trainer to help her with a foothold.'

'And it gives you the moral high ground, even though I got to the top first.' Lark turned the corners of her mouth down. 'Work tomorrow. Is it just me, or is work not quite as much fun as it used to be?'

'These changes. They're unsettling, but I guess we just have to trust that they'll work themselves out. And *home* is a great deal more fun than it used to be.'

She smiled up at him. 'That's true.'

Will's fingers brushed the back of her hand and a wave of longing crashed over Lark. He had that power over her now. Will's smallest gesture could make her forget about everything else.

'Look.' His forehead creased in thought. 'Today's been great, but we're still not happy with the way that we're being asked to change our focus, when we're already having to work hard to cover Howard's absence. I'll be on the phone first thing tomorrow, asking Sir Terence for a meeting. But in the meantime, our time's our own. Would you like to eat on the way home?'

'Not particularly. We had a huge lunch and I've been eating pastries all day...' Lark saw Will's smile broaden and knew he was on the same wavelength as she was. 'I was thinking... maybe see how things go in the dark?'

'I thought you didn't like the dark?'

'I might well change my point of view if you're there with me...'

'And you're telling me this now? With an hour's drive ahead of us.'

'We can think about it on the way home.' Lark liked teasing him. The way his blue eyes ignited with desire left her in no doubt about what Will would be thinking about on the way home.

Wordlessly, he opened the car door for her, waiting for her to get in before he hurried around to the driver's side. A couple of miles and then, as soon as they were on the motorway, the car moved steadily from the slow lane into the fast lane.

CHAPTER TWELVE

SOME MONDAYS, everything just went right. Others took a bit more work. Everyone at Migraine Community Action was beginning to miss Howard now, and Lark and Will were busy talking a variety of issues through with various members of staff. And it took four calls from Will and an email before they found out at the end of the morning that Sir Terence was on holiday for the next three weeks.

'Mexico, apparently.'

'Ah. Nice.' Lark could imagine herself on a plane to Mexico at the moment. 'I assume he's not looking at his emails.'

'Of course not. The email I sent was forwarded on to his secretary, and she called me back to say that he has a free space in his diary in a month's time.'

They were both thinking the same thing. Nothing was likely to change in the next month but Lark would bet that Pete had a few things to surprise them with before they had a chance to speak with Sir Terence. Something had to be done.

'Uma Desai?'

Will nodded. 'Yeah, in the circumstances I think it's justified. She's the Deputy Chair, and Sir Terence never let us know he was going on holiday. We're not going behind his back.'

Lark didn't much care if they were. 'Call her, Will.'

He took his phone from his jacket pocket, flipping through his contacts list until he found the number. Lark tried to return to the paperwork on her desk, but words and numbers were just a jumble of meaningless squiggles.

So much had changed in the last month. Missing Robyn and wanting to take some time out to create her own space. Managing without Howard, and all of the challenges and role-changing that had come at Sir Terence's insistence. Seeing Will at last as a lover, rather than a best friend. It hadn't been all bad—Will had given her more than she'd ever thought possible—but it *had* all been challenging.

In holding on to Will, the only piece of security in a world that was changing, was she losing herself again? Changing roles with him, learning to be like him? Was it his strength she needed or just someone to mould herself around?

'You okay?'

'Oh. Yes, just a bit tired.' Lark hadn't even noticed that Will had finished his call. 'What did Uma say?'

'She has concerns. She didn't say what they were, and I didn't press her, but something's up. She'll be in town on Wednesday, and her diary's full for most of the day, but she can make an evening meeting. So we can both see her then, after work.'

'Yeah. I'll be there.'

He shot her a look of concern. 'Are you okay? This is really good news.'

'Yes, I'm happy we're going to get to see Uma.' This sudden tiredness was a little ominous. Lark hadn't had a migraine in years, but the first signs were always this feeling of exhaustion and confusion. Maybe the last month was finally taking its toll.

'Why don't I cover this afternoon and you can go early? You look as if you need some rest.'

His concern wasn't any different to the attitude that Will had always taken. They'd always supported each other, without questions or keeping score. If one of them needed some time out, then the other covered for them. But this time,

Lark couldn't help feeling that Will had been keeping exactly the same hours that she had, and was under the same stress...

Another failure, maybe. Right now, she didn't much care. She wanted to go home so badly that all she could think about was her head hitting the pillow.

'Okay. If you don't mind.' Lark closed her laptop, putting it into her bag, along with the files she was working on.

'No problem. I'll pop in this evening to see how you are.'

Something was bothering Lark. Will knew her well enough to be sure of it, but it seemed not quite well enough for her to share, which was unusual. He told himself that she was just tired, and that the stress of the last few weeks had snapped back at her and hit her in the face.

But when he called in at her house that evening, she answered the door in her dressing gown, looking terrible. He hurried her back to bed, noticing the medication on the dressing table, along with a piece of paper that Lark had used to jot down the times she'd taken her tablets.

'You have a migraine?'

She attempted a smile. 'Yeah. Stupid, eh? I'm

busy telling everyone else how *not* to get migraines.'

'You can't avoid every single one of them. I think that's pretty standard advice as well.'

'At least I've stopped throwing up now. Think I'm on the mend.'

Her eyelids were drooping and her speech was slightly slurred. *On the mend* wasn't a description that Will would have applied, but maybe she'd been even worse during the course of the afternoon.

'Why didn't you give me a call?'

'You were taking the clinic for me. Have you only just finished?' Lark pulled at the sleeve of her dressing gown, obviously trying to find her watch, and Will noticed that it was sitting on the bedside table, next to her tablets.

'It's half past seven. And yes, I did stay a bit late, I needed to go through a few things with Dev. He was in the office and helped me with the clinic.'

'Okay. Why don't you go home, Will? I'm no good this evening.'

'That's precisely why I'm staying here. Can you remember when you took your last dose of medication?'

'Uh...' Obviously not. Will checked the paper under the blister pack on the bedside table, and since there was two hours to go before she was due another dose he put it in his pocket.

'I'm going to pop home and get some clothes for the morning. I'll only be half an hour. Would you like anything before I go?'

'Water. Please...'

Will went to the kitchen, fetching a bottle of water from the fridge and a plastic beaker. Lark drank thirstily and then flopped back onto the pillows, closing her eyes. He decided it was best to let her sleep, and picked up her front door keys from the table in the hall, letting himself out.

Lark woke early the next morning, feeling better. She vaguely remembered Will having been there last night, and now he was sleeping soundly on the other side of the bed. She cursed silently, wondering why she hadn't had the sense to send him home.

This was all wrong. Migraine again, after so many years that it was lucky her medication wasn't out of date. She sat up, finding that her head was still throbbing.

'Hey. How are you feeling?'

'Fine. Didn't I send you home last night?'

He smiled, rubbing his eyes. 'Yes. I didn't listen.'

The obscure feeling of guilt started to grow

in Lark's chest. 'That's too good of you, Will. I wasn't sick all over you, was I?'

'No. I managed to avoid that indignity. In fact, you weren't sick at all when I was here, just really sleepy.'

The vomiting must have been earlier, then. Thank goodness for that. Lark sat up in bed, feeling for the piece of paper that told her when she'd last taken her tablets, and Will's neat handwriting showed that she'd not taken any medication since half past nine the previous evening.

'You've got great writing for a doctor, Will.'

He chuckled, getting out of bed. He had great everything. Arms, legs. *Really* great eyes...

Lark leaned back against the pillows. 'I'll be okay when I've had my tablets and a cup of tea.'

'Sure you will. Yesterday you didn't even know how much medication you'd given yourself. Today you're thinking of dispensing medication to other people? You want me to examine your reflexes?'

It was a threat, and he knew it. Lark wasn't going to submit to that. 'You can't examine me, you're wearing boxer shorts. And I won't go to work today.'

'Good decision. You want me to call in for you?'

'No, I'll do it.' Lark closed her eyes. 'In a minute...'

***

By lunchtime she was feeling much better. And by the time Will got back after work the brain fog had lifted and she'd cooked him a meal.

'This looks great.' He sat down at the kitchen table. 'You cooked it yourself?'

'I went out for a walk and decided to surprise you. So I looked through some recipe cards in the supermarket and found something I liked.' Chicken and leeks in a creamy sauce, with roast potatoes and vegetables hadn't been so difficult, although she'd had to call Robyn at one point and there had been more washing-up than Lark was used to.

'You're hungry?' He nodded towards her full plate.

'I could eat a horse. That's how I know a migraine's well and truly finished, I feel wide awake and hungry.'

She waited while he tried his food. That was what Will always did when he cooked her something, and she hadn't realised what a pleasure it was to see someone take their first bite and then smile.

'That's really good. I would have gone for slightly more mustard, but that's just my preference.'

Lark tried hers. 'Yes, I think you're right…'

* * *

Slightly more mustard. Lark had had an early night, and was curled up alone in her bed. She'd told Will that she'd give the meeting with Uma a miss and he'd offered to postpone it, because he wanted her there. And Lark had shaken her head, sending him home to get a good night's sleep, because tomorrow was important to both of them.

And she was *still* thinking about mustard. The woman who never cooked, reading through recipe cards in the supermarket. Going to parties and trying to do his job better than he could. Letting him go to tomorrow's meeting alone, to speak for her, even though she knew he would, and that he'd do it well. Feeling alone now, because he wasn't here to hold her.

Perhaps that was love. And perhaps she'd just found someone else to mould herself around, the way she'd moulded herself around her parents' fears for Robyn. The migraine had been just one of those things, that happened so infrequently now it was barely a problem. But she couldn't help wondering whether the migraines she'd had as a child were because fitting a square peg into a round hole was stressful and required the kind of contortion that was bound to cause pain.

This was the first day off, spent alone and

with nothing much to do, that she'd had in over a month. It was bound to let a few crazy thoughts loose in her head, and she should ignore them. She loved Will, and he loved her.

A day at work had dispelled her doubts, or at least not allowed Lark to think about them too deeply. Will had texted at nine o'clock, saying that the meeting with Uma had been really positive and asking if she'd like him to drop round on his way home. Lark had texted back with one word—*YES*—followed by hearts and smiley faces. It was only natural that something so new, so different, would be confusing at times, and yesterday she'd not been well and not really thinking straight.

She was at the front door before Will had a chance to ring the bell. He kissed her and they sat down at the kitchen table, Lark drinking herbal tea, while Will stuck with coffee.

'So tell me everything. How did it all go?'

'Good news. Apparently Sir Terence has been less than forthcoming with the other trustees. He told them that he was managing the situation and, being busy people, they left him to it. But Uma had a feeling that something was up because so little information was getting back to her, which is why she made time to meet me straight away.'

'They didn't know?' Lark stared at him, open-mouthed. The whole point of a board of trustees was that they were a carefully chosen blend of expertise, and their remit was to make decisions collectively, supporting the work of the charity.

'Yeah, I was pretty shocked to hear that. Strictly speaking, Sir Terence has the authority to make decisions on behalf of the rest of the trustees, but only if they're unable to meet. Uma told me that he hadn't attempted to call a meeting, and that any structural changes, like appointing a temporary CEO would definitely warrant one. She didn't say too much because she needs to at least speak to the other trustees before giving us any specific answers, but she's clearly very concerned and on the case. She's going to try to call a meeting over the weekend, and if that's not possible she'll make sure that at least she's spoken to everyone before Monday.'

'Good. That's really good news, Will.' Lark felt a weight lifting from her shoulders. Maybe they could start to get back to something like normal now. 'So hopefully Pete won't be dreaming up any new hoops for us to jump through on Friday.'

'I made sure that it didn't sound as if I was giving Uma a list of demands, but that was the one thing I *did* ask her for. I said that the sessions with Pete, and what he was asking of us, was taking up a lot of our time, and that while personal growth is something we're always up for, we're struggling to keep our heads above water right now. She agreed, got him on the phone straight away and cancelled the sessions until further notice.'

'Oh! That's a relief.' Lark felt tears prick at the sides of her eyes. 'Some of the things he was saying were valid but...'

Will's gaze softened. 'I didn't learn too much from him. I learned a lot from you, and those are the things I'll take with me from the last couple of weeks.'

That was nice. Pete had insisted that they break out of their roles, but all that had happened was she'd felt forced into another role, one that she felt uncomfortable with. Now, perhaps, she could take a breath, and start to reclaim her own space again. Find a place where she and Will could grow together.

'Uma didn't give me any assurances, but she did ask how we would prefer to organise things while Howard's away.' There was a sudden hesitancy in his voice.

'And...?'

'I told her that we both feel that things should stay as they are for the time being. Appointing one of us as a temporary CEO isn't necessary, and it's an unneeded complication. We function best as a team.'

'Uma agreed to that?'

'Until the trustees have had a chance to consult with each other, and us, to make a decision. She said that we do need some kind of plan about what happens next if Howard either can't or doesn't want to return.'

'I don't want to think about that.' The quiver in Lark's stomach wasn't solely out of concern for Howard. There was something Will wasn't telling her.

'Neither do I. But Uma made it clear that if it does become necessary to appoint a new CEO, that she personally would like to see either you or I take the job.'

'No. Will, that's putting us right back into the same position that Sir Terence put us in.'

'We talked about that, and I'm sure that's not Uma's intention, but we do have to be practical.' His chest rose and fell as he took a breath. 'I've told her that if that does become necessary, then I'm not interested in the position.'

'What? Will…' Lark stared at him. 'We haven't talked about that.'

'No, we haven't. But that's my decision, I feel that the best way forward for the charity is with you as CEO.'

'But…'

'You're a versatile and talented medical professional, you inspire people and you make things happen. They'd be crazy not to pick you.'

'And so...you made that decision for me?' Lark felt as if she'd just been submerged in cold water. Suddenly she was fighting for breath, her heart thumping.

'No, I made the decision that I wanted to stand aside. Are you telling me you don't want the job?'

Who wouldn't want it? The chance to steer a place she loved, to make a real difference. Not like this, though. 'Are you telling me that *you* don't?'

He grinned suddenly. That blue-eyed smile that could charm the birds from the trees. 'I did tell you that I thought I'd rather enjoy working under you...'

He had, and when they'd put that into practice it'd had nothing to do with work.

'Don't flirt with me, Will. I seem to remember that I said I didn't much want to have to deal with Sir Terence on my own.'

'From what Uma says, I'd be willing to bet that's not going to happen. She was noting down a list of points, things where you and I felt that our ability to do our jobs well had been compromised, and where Sir Terence had ignored proper procedures. I didn't ask, because she obviously didn't want to say, but I'm sure she'll be taking those to the other trustees. You're the best person for the job, Lark, and I don't think that Sir Terence is going to be getting in your way.'

'So you're just going to back off, are you? You're not thinking straight, Will, the charity needs someone like you at the helm. But this isn't about that. It's about you making a decision about my life without asking me first.'

He couldn't see it. A look of annoyance showed in his face, before it was quickly hidden. 'If you didn't want me to make decisions, why did you ask me to go alone? But that's okay, I'll call Uma in the morning and tell her that I want to compete with you for the CEO's post. Because that's worked so well for us so far.'

'What exactly *has* worked for us, Will?'

He shrugged in frustration. 'You don't know?'

Lark knew. For the last few weeks, she'd had a lover who was a friend. Someone who she could show her own life to, and who had shown his in return. It had been wonderful, but even that wasn't enough, if she couldn't find herself.

'I wanted to create my own space, where I could find out who I am. Everything seemed so uncertain and I clung on to you…' The enormity of what she'd done hit Lark. Will didn't deserve this. 'I was your friend, and I tried to mould myself into something else. Someone who could change roles with you at work and who could be a part of your life.'

'Is there anything wrong with that? I did the same, and... I know you better now. I think I know myself better.' Will seemed at a loss, suddenly. Beneath all of his charm, he was a kind, careful man, and Lark wondered whether he could even begin to appreciate what she was talking about.

'You have a place in the world, Will. You know who you are. I'm not sure that I have any idea who I am, I just feel pulled backwards and forwards, as if I have no real anchor.'

'By me, you mean?' His face darkened. 'Pulled back and forth by me?'

She couldn't deny it. But that wasn't Will's fault, he'd never asked her to do anything, let alone pulled her. 'It's me, Will. Not you.'

Chagrin showed in his face. *It isn't you, it's me.* Maybe he'd said that a few times, to nameless women, who Lark had never paid too much attention to because she'd known that Will's relationships never lasted. This must be new to him, someone who couldn't hold down a relationship as long as he could.

'I'm in this for keeps, Lark. I always have been, ever since we first became friends, and I couldn't imagine a time when we wouldn't be there for each other. And when we became lovers…' He shook his head. 'I can't even say how much you mean to me. I don't have the words.'

She loved him too. And that was the problem, because there was no going back from it now, no return to that easy friendship that they'd both valued so much. She'd given herself to Will before she'd really worked out who she was and what she wanted in life, and that had made the gift worth nothing.

She realised that she'd been staring at him silently, and that Will had been waiting for her to say something. When she didn't, because she honestly didn't know what to say, he said it for her.

'We've got a decision to make, haven't we.'

He was braver than she was. He always had been.

'Yes, we do.'

'You have to tell me what you want, Lark. Whatever that is, we can work out a way to keep the charity running. The one thing I won't have is for you to be unhappy and feel you don't have a way out.'

'You're an honourable man, Will.'

'And that's not an answer.'

He was hurting, that was obvious. And Lark owed him an answer, even if it hurt her to give it. 'We have to stop. *I* have to stop, before I tear us both into little pieces.'

It was all breaking apart. Four years of relying on each other and a few short weeks that had been sweeter than anything that Lark could imagine, even if they'd ultimately proved to be the catalyst that separated them. Lark swallowed down her tears, knowing that she needed to go through with this, if only to save a great deal more hurt later on.

And there were no words. The ones that they always used—*See you later...tomorrow...on Monday. Have a good weekend...a good evening...a great holiday*—suddenly they had no future.

'I'll...' The words died in her throat, because Lark had no idea what she was going to do next.

'Yeah. I'll miss you too.' Will had the courage to make that sound like the ending that Lark couldn't quite get her head around yet. Or maybe he just had more experience with endings…

Not fair. She was the one who was saying goodbye, not him. And Lark didn't even know how to say it. But Will knew how to leave. He got to his feet, picking up his coat and briefcase, and walked away.

CHAPTER THIRTEEN

LIFE. IN ALL its rich variety, its careless cruelty, and all of the moments that couldn't be taken back. Will had flagged down a taxi, and in fifteen minutes he was back home, slumped on the sofa, staring at the wall. Then he tried out a little pacing, while he formed the words that he hadn't been able to say to Lark.

We can work this out.

They couldn't. Lark needed some space to work out what she really wanted in life, after having put her parents' fears before her own needs for so long. He needed to be able to untangle the complex web that had been spun around them, the roles that had been questioned and changed in both their work lives and their personal lives, and to find something solid to hold on to. But the more he thought about it, the more he felt that there *was* nothing to hold on to, and he was just groping in the darkness.

I love you.

Of course he did. Not loving Lark was beyond his capabilities, but it didn't make any difference. He should have taken what he had, and when the temptation to want more had seized him he should have resisted it. Hadn't he already resolved that he'd never again put himself into the position of having to lose someone who was everything to him?

Don't do this, Lark...

That was the most outrageous proposition of all. Letting go was all he knew how to do now, and Lark needed someone who would fight for her. He hadn't fought tonight, and he wasn't going to go back and do it tomorrow or the next day. Losing her had flipped a switch somewhere deep inside him, and he couldn't go back and risk doing it all over again.

Pacing really wasn't doing any good. He could keep it up all night, and still not find the answers he was looking for. There were a few invitations propped up on the mantelpiece, all of which he'd politely declined in favour of spending time with Lark, painting different coloured squares on her kitchen wall. Maybe a little bland conversation, saying everything and meaning nothing, was what he'd be needing in the days and weeks ahead.

* * *

Howard's sister, Petra, was a nice woman, clearly worried for him and trying hard to restore as much normality to the situation as she could. Alyssa had phoned Will, going round the houses until she got to the point of her call. If it wasn't too inconvenient, and he didn't mind...

Yes, he'd be there, and Alyssa should take Sunday afternoon for herself, as usual. Not being able to get a word in edgeways didn't normally bother Howard too much, but it had gained a new meaning recently, and Will would try to steer things in the direction of the new normal.

Petra looked around at the plants and the tall windows, which made the visitors' room light and airy. 'It's very nice here, isn't it? Now that you can walk it must be so much easier to make friends.'

Howard nodded.

'I suppose I'd better go now, though. I wish I could spend some more time with you, but just seeing you looking so well is an enormous relief.'

Howard *did* look well. That wasn't his problem. The twist of his lips was masked by the slight droop on one side of his face.

'It's such a long drive...' Petra looked at her

watch. 'Next time, maybe I'll stay overnight with Alyssa, and we can have a really good talk.'

Howard opened his mouth to speak, but only managed a few jumbled, incoherent sounds. Clearly the idea was engendering a strong emotion, which made it more difficult for him to concentrate and form the words he needed. Will saw a slight movement of Howard's left hand, the familiar over-to-you gesture that he used in business meetings.

'Everyone appreciates your having come so far. I know that Alyssa's been struggling to find some time to herself and she's been able to relax this afternoon, knowing you're here to visit.' Will tried to tactfully steer Petra away from the idea.

'Of course. We all need a little me time.' Petra nodded sympathetically. 'Maybe I shouldn't bother her. I could send her a box of fruit or some flowers, perhaps. Or something for the bath...'

'Good idea!' Automatic speech—the everyday phrases that were said without thinking—was often unimpaired by aphasia and it was sometimes startling to hear Howard speak so fluently. Even Will jumped a little, and Petra's face was a picture of astonished delight.

'That's what I'll do then, Howard. A bath before bedtime with a few favourite luxuries always helps me sleep...' She was chattering nineteen to the dozen again, and Howard seemed to relax a little. Goodbyes were said, kisses were blown in Howard's direction and then suddenly the room fell silent.

Will waited. Howard was making the difficult connections between thought and the physical process of speech, and no doubt he'd be saying what was on his mind when he was ready.

'She...means...well.' The three words were carefully modulated. Howard's therapist had been teaching him to slow down and space his words out, beating time with his hand. The technique was clearly working.

'She seems very concerned for you.' Will supplied the words that he guessed Howard might be looking for. 'Maybe a little too much of the talking *at* you and not *with* you?'

Howard rolled his eyes and nodded. Sometimes actions did speak louder than words.

'Anything you want me to do?' Will waved his hand, dismissing his last question as far too broad. 'Sorry. Would you like me to get someone to mention that she needs to give you a bit more time to put what you want to say together? Kindly, of course, so as not to hurt her feelings.'

Howard nodded. He didn't get away with that with the staff here, they'd wait until he answered, even if it was just a *yes*. 'You...'

'You'd like *me* to call her? Maybe give her an update on your therapy and the techniques they're using to help you speak again?'

'Yes!'

Automatic speech again. Will had heard it before, many times, but he was still getting used to hearing it from a friend. Those sudden glimpses of how Howard had spoken before the stroke, when now he had to struggle to frame his words.

'Okay. I'll speak to Alyssa and get her number. Now that she's seen you I'm sure she has a lot of questions, and I'll do what I can to answer them.' Howard had no doubt thought all of this through already. It was a fine line between putting words into his mouth and checking that Will understood his intentions properly, but this time the process worked and Howard nodded.

'And I'll be tactful.'

Howard gave a short laugh, his raised eyebrow saying that he'd expect nothing less from Will. Tact. Kindness. Making out that everything was okay, even though his own life felt as if it were falling apart. He and Lark made copious use of email, but he hadn't actually laid eyes on her for the last two weeks. The gnawing pain seemed worse every day, and Will knew from experience that it wasn't going to get better any time soon.

A smiling nurse wheeled a tea trolley towards them. 'Would you like a drink, Howard?'

The nurses here knew exactly how to approach each patient. Every stroke was different, and each person had different physical or cognitive damage to contend with. Howard could deal with one question at a time much better than a whole string of choices.

'Yes. Thank you.' Howard got the words out and smiled up at the nurse.

'Tea or coffee, then?'

'Tea…' Howard clearly wasn't finished yet and the nurse waited quietly. 'Thank you, Marie.'

He got a luminous grin in return. 'Nice one, Howard, you're welcome. One cup of tea coming up. You want something, Will?'

'Tea would be great, thank you.'

Biscuits were offered and accepted, and Marie gave a cheery wave as she wheeled the trolley out of the room. No doubt the next person would be expected to practise whatever skills their stroke had robbed them of, as well.

'How is…work?' Clearly, the matter was of some importance to Howard and he'd been practising the phrase.

'I thought we'd decided that you could do with a break from that, Howard.' Will shot him a reproachful look, and got one back in return.

'Okay. You're not going to stop wondering, just because I don't talk to you about it, are you?'

Howard shook his head pointedly.

'In that case...' Will wondered whether *Everything's fine* might wash, and decided it wouldn't. 'Lark and I are taking one day at a time. We've been through everything that was on your desk and it's just whatever comes in, now. I'm not sure either of us realised just how much you deal with in the course of a working day, but we're managing.'

'Any...questions?'

'Not at the moment. But we'll ask if we do have any. Is that okay?'

Howard nodded emphatically. Maybe the strategy of not bothering him with anything that was going on at work was beginning to outlive its usefulness. He was kept pretty busy with his therapy, and fatigue was a normal after-effect of a stroke, but Will imagined that he would have concerns about his work too, if he were in Howard's shoes.

'All right. I'll email Lark and we'll get together a list of questions...' Will amended the thought. 'One of her famous yes/no decision sheets, maybe.'

'Yes. Good.' That seemed to satisfy Howard, but when Will opened his mouth to reply he waved his hand impatiently. There was more, obviously.

'You...' Howard grimaced, struggling for words that wouldn't come. 'Email?'

Right. There was clearly nothing wrong with Howard's perceptive abilities, and Will found himself wishing that they didn't have to go in this direction.

'Yeah. We've both been pretty busy, naturally, and we're finding that being in the office on different days has helped. I haven't seen much of her in the last couple of weeks.' For that, read *nothing*. Now Will was groping in the dark for the right words, because the idea of living without Lark left him wondering how he could make any sense of his future.

Howard nodded, taking a sip of his tea. 'Trustees...?'

Yeah. Good question. Happily, things seemed to have settled a bit on that front. 'They've been great. Sir Terence is looking to explore other avenues at the moment, and Uma's taken over as Chair of the Board. She's been great, really supportive of both of us.'

The mention of Uma Desai's name mollified Howard a little. Clearly he'd been wondering exactly what was going on, and the suspicion that he'd done more to protect him and Lark than they ever knew solidified into certainty.

'Don't...' Howard frowned, lost for words again, and then shook his head.

'We can come back to that.' Will leaned back in his chair, picking up his tea. Relaxing and then coming back to what he wanted to say often seemed to help.

But Howard didn't want to let go of the thought just yet. He picked up the pencil and pad that lay on the table next to him and started to write, then scribbled the words out angrily when he saw that they weren't making any sense. Yet another of the effects of the stroke—Howard could read with understanding and, being left-handed, he could manipulate a pencil, but the aphasia prevented him from writing coherently.

'Do...not...allow...any...' Howard paused and Will waited. 'Nothing...to...get...in...the... way.'

The careful separation of each word seemed to give particular emphasis to them, and they hit Will with such force that he almost dropped his teacup. As usual, Howard had thought about the situation and got right to the heart of it.

'You mean between Lark and me?' That was Howard's obvious meaning, but this time Will needed to confirm it for himself.

'Yes.'

'We shouldn't allow anything else to get in

the way of our friendship, you mean?' It was good advice, but sadly a little late.

Howard nodded, reaching for his tea, but Will couldn't let this go.

'You're talking about the trustees?'

Howard shrugged. 'Any... Nothing.'

Clearly he was having difficulties with the word *anything*. But Will had the message, loud and clear. Howard knew them both well, and his insights had helped them to use their different approaches to good effect when they'd first begun to work together.

And it was a good thought. Will's past, Lark's past. The different roles that everyone had expected them to take, and which they'd obligingly clung to. All of the things that he needed now, and the things he'd tried to give Lark but hadn't been able to. If you took them out of the equation was there somewhere, a quiet place at the centre of it all, where they could meet?

It was too big a thought to be able to put anything into words. And Howard had said what he'd made his mind up to say, and seemed content now.

'Thanks for the advice. I'll make sure to act on it...'

CHAPTER FOURTEEN

LARK HAD BEEN FUNCTIONING. For the last two weeks she'd kept on top of her work commitments, and that was really all she needed to do. Going out wasn't something she'd done all that much in the past. In fact, it had usually been Robyn who had dragged her out for the evening.

Functioning was a good word for it. Numb, unthinking, like a cog in a massive machine. Trying not to think about Will, or how much it hurt to be apart from him, because she was sure that was the right thing to do. She'd written him a carefully worded email and he'd returned an equally carefully worded one. The roles that they'd both taken on had been smashed, and they couldn't be together while they were both beginning to explore what that meant. They should remain friends.

The last part of that was a piece of blue-sky optimism on both their parts. Friends would be an agonising reminder of all they'd lost. At the moment, even seeing Will's name on her email list made her heart jump, and seeing him would be far too much to bear. Their fragile working relationship needed to continue, for the time being, anyway. But Lark had already explored the possibility of increasing her hours working as an ambulance paramedic, and as soon as Migraine Community Action didn't need her any more she'd be gone. There would be no working over Will, or under him, or next to him.

Robyn and Matt drove down for one of their semi-regular Sunday meet-ups, and her sister looked around the sitting room, grinning.

'Love the new colours. Very you. Warm and soothing...'

'And bold.' Matt added his opinion.

'Yeah, definitely bold,' Robyn agreed.

'You think so?' The warm and soothing part fitted in with Lark's picture of herself, but she'd never reckoned on bold. Of the two of them, bold more nearly described Robyn.

'Absolutely. I wouldn't think of painting a sitting room this colour, but now that I can see it it's stupendous. When did you have the time to do all this? I know you've been pretty busy at work.'

'Will helped me.' The words slipped out before Lark could stop them. That was the trouble with actually talking to people face to face, her ever-present thoughts about Will were a lot more difficult to disguise.

'No!' Robyn yelped in amusement. 'You mean you had that gorgeous hunk of manhood in your sitting room in a pair of overalls?'

'Hey! Do I have to worry?' Matt grinned.

'Of course not. He's not my type.' Robyn shot her new husband a dazzling smile. 'You're my type. And you're great with a paintbrush as well.'

'Thank you.' Matt looked around the room again. 'Does this mean we'll be getting the paint charts out again when we get home?'

'No, because our colours say it all about us. That gorgeous green that you didn't think was going to work in the sitting room but we had it because I wanted it. And the blue that you chose for the hall, which I didn't think I'd be able to bear, but I've discovered I rather like it after all. They're proof positive that we're madly in love, because we'd never have said yes to them for any other reason.'

Matt thought for a moment. 'True. Good point.'

'And Lark's colours are bold and brave. With a lot of warmth.'

'Bold's not me, Robyn.' Lark tried to laugh the idea off. It hurt, because if she'd been bolder then maybe she could have cut through her uncertainties and fears, and found a way to stay with Will.

'But it is. Really. You're a paramedic and you help run a charity. You've written academic papers and...' Robyn reached for Lark's hand. 'I couldn't have achieved half of what I've been able to do without you.'

'That's not true. Your achievements belong to you, not me.'

'You didn't see what it was like at home, Lark. Mum and Dad were so fearful, and there was so much conflict, so many arguments. And then, remember that weekend when you turned up, sat everyone down at the kitchen table and gave us a plan that we could all live with? That was a way forward for me, and one for Mum and Dad as well, only it took them longer to really come to terms with it. I reckoned that if you could be that bold, then I could stop listening to all of Mum and Dad's fears, and be bold too.'

'I... I don't know what to say...' Lark reached over to hug her sister.

'Have I said the wrong thing?'

'No. It was the right thing, and I'm happy that you feel that way.' It was too late though. The time for being bold, for believing in herself and hanging on to the love she'd lost, was gone now.

'Um...' She heard Matt clear his throat.

'Sorry to interrupt... But is the oven meant to be smoking like that?'

'No!' Robyn yelped, and Matt sprang to his feet and hurried into the kitchen. Smoke plumed upwards as he opened the oven door, and he drew out the casserole dish that contained their lunch, carefully peeling back the foil lid.

'I think that's... I can't actually tell what it is, but it's beyond saving. Perhaps I should open a window.' Matt turned the corners of his mouth down.

'Never mind. We'll go out for lunch, shall we? My treat.' Robyn grinned.

The heavy despair that had been weighing Lark down seemed to lift suddenly. 'Yes, let's do that. There's a new place next door to the coffee shop we used to go to that I've been meaning to try...'

Bold. It was the kind of word that could change a life, and when Robyn and Matt had left Lark was still turning it over in her head. She sat down at the kitchen table and opened her laptop, the impulse to reach out impossible to ignore.

Then she saw it. Before she'd had a chance to think, she'd clicked on Will's name in the list of unread emails. The message wasn't a long one, just two paragraphs inviting her to meet with him next weekend. He thought that lunch, somewhere out of town, might be easier for both of them.

It was the first time that either of them had alluded to anything being easier, because that implied that it might be hard. And for Will, the man who always tried to make out that everything was okay, it was practically outrageous. She snapped her laptop shut, as if that might create some distance between her and the email and allow her to breathe again.

Bold. She opened the laptop again, staring at Will's email. Then typed a few lines, saying that she thought a meeting would be a good idea, and did he have any thoughts about where they might do it. Then she read it over twice and pressed *send* before she had a chance to read it again for a third time.

Will wouldn't be sitting watching his email on a Sunday evening, and there was no point in staring at the screen waiting. Lark walked over to the coffee machine and then decided that she wanted tea and flipped the kettle on. Over the bubble of boiling water she heard the distinctive ping that announced she had new mail.

She wouldn't even look. It was just another spam email. But when Lark returned to the screen to shut her laptop down, there was Will's name again, right at the top of the list.

Tunbridge Wells station at noon on Saturday.

It was a bit of a trek, but getting right out of London seemed sensible. Whatever happened in Tunbridge Wells probably stayed there, and if something *did* go wrong then they could leave that behind them.

Her fingers shaking, she typed a line to say that the time and place sounded good, and that she'd be there. Then Lark closed her laptop and put it away in a drawer in the sitting room where she couldn't see it. Even so, visions of Tunbridge Wells were circling her thoughts like a pack of lions…

The week had been ordinary. Will's emails had been just the same, pleasant and businesslike, and Lark's replies had been the same. She'd spent an inordinate amount of time thinking about what to wear on Saturday, and then he'd emailed and said that he had somewhere in mind that involved a short walk, and that a pair of sturdy shoes might be in order. Lark decided not to ask, and that jeans and a nice top would probably be more appropriate than the dress she'd had in mind.

She'd missed breakfast and spent the whole of the train journey to Tunbridge Wells staring at the pastry she'd bought at the station, and telling herself that it was okay to feel nervous, but she mustn't show it when she met Will.

He was leaning against his car in the station car park. Jeans that fitted like a glove and a dark blue sweater, which would no doubt complement the colour of his eyes perfectly when she got close enough to see them. But she had to forget all of that, because suddenly Lark knew exactly why she was here. Loving Will meant that she wanted him to be happy, and she had to be bold enough to fight for his future, whatever it might cost her.

Will smiled, looking uncharacteristically nervous, and she smiled back. He opened the car door, and Lark got in. They drove in silence, taking the main road out of the town and then upwards towards the top of one of the surrounding hills.

'Such a lovely view.' Perhaps he was heading for a restaurant on the look-out point that was signposted up ahead.

'Yeah. It's nice to get out of town sometimes.' Will smiled suddenly, as if he'd been wondering whether that was permissible. On the whole, Lark would rather he didn't as it made her stomach do a sudden loop-the-loop.

'Yes, it is. And it's a beautiful clear day.'

The reference to the weather silenced both of them. The road dwindled into a one-lane track and Will pulled to one side, onto a small hardstanding area at the top. Lark got out, looking around. There was a large cairn of stones, which marked the look-out, and a few benches. Apart from a couple of dog-walkers, trudging to the top of the hill and then turning to go back down again, it was deserted.

'We have to walk?'

Will had ducked back into the car, grabbing a zipped backpack. 'No, we're here.'

Okay. Lark followed him over to the bench that was furthest from the footpath that led up to the beacon and when he sat down she did so too, leaving as much space as she could between them.

The strong breeze seemed to pull at her, taking the city air from her lungs and replacing it with something fresher. Tugging at her hair, making Lark feel that she wanted to shake her head and knock out all the cobwebs that had formed. It was nice, but she was sure that wasn't what they were here for.

'I thought of making a booking at a quiet restaurant…' Will was looking at her intently, displaying none of the easy charm that had become his hallmark. 'But I wanted to bring you somewhere like this. I hope you don't mind.'

'It's nice. Refreshing.'

'And it's just the two of us.'

Alone with Will. Those moments in the night when he'd seemed like the only person in the world. Lark ruthlessly drove the thought from her mind.

'That's good. We can talk here.'

'I was hoping so.' Will took a deep breath. 'Just you and me, Lark. Nothing from the past, nothing from our families or our work. Maybe here we can find out what's really keeping us apart...'

She was staring at him, wide-eyed. The sun chose that moment to come out from behind a cloud, and Will was suddenly bathed in the golden gaze that he loved so very dearly. It gave him the courage to press on.

'I walked away from you without putting up a fight, and that was wrong of me. Because all we are, all we've ever done, is meet problems head-on and solve them together.'

'Because we're different, Will. Two points of view is better than just one in a work situation.'

'I don't accept that. How could I love you the way I do if we didn't have the same goals, the same way of looking at things?'

Too much. He'd said the word, and meant it, and he couldn't take it back now. A tear rolled down Lark's cheek.

'Don't say that, Will. Please.' There was pain in her voice, but that gave Will hope. If she couldn't love him then there would be no pain, and she probably wouldn't be sitting here next to him.

'Okay, I won't say it again. And if you want to go home I'll take you back to the station, whenever you say the word. But if you'll stay and fight for what we have, then here's the place to do it. Just you and me, with nothing and no one else.'

She was staring out across the magnificent view of the countryside that the hilltop afforded, although Will doubted that she could see much of it because Lark's eyes were full of tears.

'Robyn told me that I was bold, the other day.'

'That's the way I've always thought of you. You have a bold heart, Lark.'

She turned towards him, and Will saw something ignite in her eyes. 'We were wrong, Will. We let go of what we had without a fight. You've got coffee in that bag?' She nodded at the backpack that he'd put between them on the bench.

'Yes.' He fumbled with the zip, trying not to hope too much. 'And sandwiches.'

'Okay. I'll take the coffee. And then we'll do battle, shall we?'

They'd talked for hours. Broken it all down. They'd both struggled against the confines of the roles they'd found themselves in, but it had been difficult to let them go. Admitting that he was human wasn't quite so hard, because Lark had admitted she was human too. They'd made mistakes, and they'd been hurt.

But they could both move on from that. They could leave the hurt and the mistakes behind, and make new lives. Fresh and clean as a hilltop on a summer's day, always remembering the past but never being bound by it.

Will was falling in love all over again. With a bold, complex woman, who was fighting every step of the way. Finally, they were alone. Sitting on a bench together, with nothing to come between them.

Lark was silent for what seemed an age. And then she turned to him. 'I love you, Will.'

He'd promised he wouldn't say it again, but it was the only thing he wanted to tell Lark. Will hesitated and she grinned suddenly. 'You can say it if you want to now.'

'I love you, Lark. I want to love you every day...' Maybe it was a little too soon to mention the rest of his life.

'We'll keep each other honest, eh?' She leaned forward and kissed his cheek. It took Will's breath away.

'That was...'

'Different. Special...'

'Nothing between us...'

She smiled, laying her hand on his shoulder. 'You can kiss me back. If you want to.'

It was all that Will wanted. More than he'd even known he might want. 'I love you, Lark. I'll love you always.'

She gave him that brilliant, golden smile of hers. 'That's good, because I'm going to love you always too. Starting now.'

All he wanted was to feel her close. Suddenly bringing her here, to the top of a hill that was miles from home, didn't seem such a great idea. But for now, being here with Lark, feeling his heart open and fill the space that had previously contained only doubts…

'How long does it take to get back home by car?' Lark grinned up at him.

'A while. But I have an admission to make. I wasn't sure how this afternoon was going to go, and if it went badly… I didn't want you to have to choose between going home late on the train or having to take a lift from me.'

'So—let me get this right. You considered the possibility that we'd be arguing until we didn't have any breath left, and then I'd be stranded here and have to accept a lift from you. Which I might not want to do.' She kissed him again. 'And you planned for it. Will, that's so sweet of you. What did you do?'

'I booked a room in your name at a hotel, close to the station. It's all paid up for the night.'

'I've got a hotel room?' She flung her arms around his neck, kissing him again. 'Will, I just happen to have a hotel room. Would you consider coming back there with me?'

EPILOGUE

Six months later

TUNBRIDGE WELLS. Everyone had to have a special place, and Tunbridge Wells was theirs. It was two days before Christmas, and everything was beginning to shut down. Lark had booked a room in a small hotel she knew, close to Tunbridge Wells station.

'This is nice.' Will lay on the bed, his hands behind his head. 'A day to ourselves before we plunge into sharing our Christmas with two different families.'

'Your mum and dad aren't going to mind us turning up on Boxing Day and missing Christmas with them?' Lark was sitting in front of the mirror, applying her make-up, ready for a special dinner that Will had booked.

'No. Wait until you see the party they have planned for New Year. They're pretty happy that we'll be making that.'

'Good. It was nice of Howard and the trustees to insist that we take time off together over Christmas.' Lark turned, resting her arm on the back of her chair. She could spend any amount of time just looking at Will. 'Nothing's going to go wrong, is it?'

'Nothing. You've planned everything with your customary skill, and everyone knows exactly what they're supposed to be doing. Uma's approved the plan and she's even put herself on the list of people who'll accept a call. That's a first for the Chair of the Board of Trustees.'

'She's such a breath of fresh air. I have a good feeling about the charity's future.'

Sir Terence had resigned, after the other trustees had confronted him about a number of things he'd been keeping from them, and his general high-handedness. Howard was back at work part-time, and was improving every day. Recovery was a long road, but it was good to see how he thrived in the atmosphere of the charity's offices, where everyone gave him time to say what was on his mind. He'd proposed that he, Will and Lark would steer the charity into the future together, and that when he finally did retire they'd take over. But no one expected that he'd be stepping back just yet, there was still more for him to do.

'That's enough about work.' Will seemed

to know what she was thinking. 'We're officially on our first holiday for six months. No one wants to hear from us until the New Year.'

'Best Christmas present ever.' Lark watched as he got up from the bed, buttoning his shirt and putting on his tie and jacket. 'Just you and me.'

'I have an idea.' He grinned at her. 'I'll need you to stand up, though.'

'So that when I fall into a swoon at the audacity of it, you can catch me?' Lark teased him, putting on her shoes and getting to her feet.

'You look so beautiful.' His hand skimmed the dark blue material of her dress.

'Is that the idea?' Lark stood on her toes to kiss him. 'I'd like to modify it a bit and include you in the definition.'

His blue eyes darkened suddenly and Will fell to one knee in front of her. 'That's not the idea, sweetheart.'

Lark's hand flew to her mouth. 'Is this... Will, is this what I think it is?' They'd talked about the future, made plans even, but this was different. Suddenly that future was here and now...

He reached into his pocket, taking out a ring that flashed in the light. 'Lark, will you marry me?'

'Yes...'

'That's not the whole plan. I want to love you for the rest of my life.'

'I'll love you too, Will. And we'll have children?'

'Absolutely. They were the next item on the list. They'll have your brains and...your looks as well.'

'They'll have our love, Will. That's what they'll really need.'

His eyes took on an imploring look. They were both shaking, and Lark hung onto his hand, knowing that Will would always be there for her.

'I only need one word. Say yes.'

'Yes, Will. Yes to everything that we can do together, for the rest of our lives.'

'Do you like the ring?' A note of uncertainty sounded in his voice.

She'd barely noticed it, because his eyes were so much more lustrous. But Lark held out her hand, and when he slipped it onto her finger the three diamonds sparkled.

'It's beautiful, Will.' She pulled him to his feet so that she could kiss him.

They'd made a promise and everything had changed. All of the things they'd talked about were no longer just hopes and dreams but had become real and tangible. Will's kisses were even more precious now.

'You're ready to go and celebrate?'

'Yes. And it'll be a definite yes for champagne, just in case you're wondering.'

Will kissed her. 'So it's *yes* to everything tonight, is it? Should I take advantage?'

'No.'

He chuckled. 'At last. I was beginning to worry that you were going to give me carte blanche on every idea I come up with.'

'Just keep coming up with ideas like this one, Will. Then I'll keep on saying *yes*.' This was rapidly shaping up to be the best night of Lark's life. And unless she was very much mistaken, there would be many more to come…

* * * * *

If you enjoyed this story, check out these other great reads from Annie Claydon

One Summer in Sydney
Children's Doc to Heal Her Heart
Cinderella in the Surgeon's Castle
Snowbound with Her Off-Limits GP

All available now!